to the Thomas Ford Memorial Library

THE BLOOD OF AN ENGLISHMAN

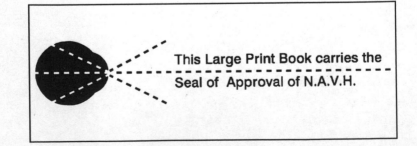

This Large Print Book carries the
Seal of Approval of N.A.V.H.

AN AGATHA RAISIN MYSTERY

THE BLOOD OF AN ENGLISHMAN

M. C. BEATON

THORNDIKE PRESS
A part of Gale, Cengage Learning

GALE
CENGAGE Learning·

Farmington Hills, Mich • San Francisco • New York • Waterville, Maine
Meriden, Conn • Mason, Ohio • Chicago

GALE
CENGAGE Learning°

LIBRARY OF CONGRESS CATALOGING-IN-PUBLICATION DATA

Beaton, M. C.
    The blood of an Englishman : an Agatha Raisin mystery / M. C. Beaton. —
Large print edition.
        pages cm. — (Thorndike Press large print mystery)
        ISBN 978-1-4104-6977-9 (hardcover) — ISBN 1-4104-6977-8 (hardcover)
        1. Raisin, Agatha (Fictitious character)—Fiction. 2. Women private
investigators—Fiction. 3. Amateur theater—Fiction. 4. City and town
life—Fiction. 5. Cotswold Hills (England)—Fiction. 6. Large type books.
I. Title.
PR6053.H4535B58 2014b
823'.914—dc23   2014033698

Published in 2014 by arrangement with St. Martin's Press, LLC

Printed in the United States of America
1 2 3 4 5 6 7 18 17 16 15 14

This book is for Tony Lee (Hot Dog)
with affection.

CHAPTER ONE

"Fee, fie, fo, fum. I smell the blood of an Englishman."

As the giant ogre in the Winter Parva pantomime strutted across the stage, uttering the old familiar words, Agatha Raisin stifled a yawn. She loathed amateur dramatics, but had been persuaded to support the pantomime by her friend, Mrs. Bloxby, the vicar's wife. The two women were in odd contrast: Agatha with her smart clothes and glossy brown hair, Mrs. Bloxby in faded tweeds and wispy brown hair streaked with grey surrounding her gentle face.

Agatha began to feel sulky and trapped. Why was she, a private detective of some fame, wasting her sweetness on the desert air of the Winter Parva village hall?

The pantomime was *Babes in the Woods*, but there were also characters from other pantomimes from *Old Mother Hubbard* to *Puss in Boots*.

At last the interval arrived. There was no theatre bar but mulled wine was being served in the entrance hall. Agatha grabbed a glass and said, "Going outside for a cigarette."

Fog lay heavily on the car park and water dripped mournfully from the trees surrounding it. "Still smoking? Dear me," said a voice behind Agatha. She swung round and found herself looking down at the gossip of her home village, Carsely, Mrs. Arnold.

"Yes," said Agatha curtly.

"Do you know that only twenty percent of the people in Britain now smoke?" said Mrs. Arnold.

"I never believe in statistics," said Agatha. "Have they asked everyone?" She surveyed Mrs. Arnold's small round figure. "Anyway, what about overeating? What about a ban on *fat* people?"

A tall man loomed up out of the mist. "What do you think of the show?"

Agatha bit back the word *hellish* that had risen to her lips and said instead, "I think the chap playing the ogre is very good. Who is he?"

"That's our local baker, Bert Simple. I haven't introduced myself. I recognise you. I'm Gareth Craven, producer of the show.

That's the end of the interval. I'd better get backstage."

"I'm Agatha Raisin," Agatha called after him.

Quite tasty, thought Agatha, watching his tall figure disappear into the fog. Well, hullo hormones, I thought you had laid down and died.

She shuffled along her seat beside Mrs. Bloxby. The hall smelled of damp people, mulled wine, and chocolates. A surprising number had brought boxes of chocolates. Pen lights flickered, voices murmured things like, "I don't want a hard one. Are those liqueur chocolates, you naughty man!" Children, used to slumping on comfortable sofas in front of the television, screamed and hit each other.

The curtains were drawn back and the comedian came on. "Hullo, hullo, hullo!" he yelled.

"Goodbye, goodbye, goodbye," muttered Agatha.

The comedian was a local man, George Southern, who owned a gift shop in the village.

He was slightly built and rather camp with thin brown hair and a large nose which overshadowed his small mouth.

"I hope you're in good voice tonight, folks," he said. A screen came down behind him. It's the compulsory sing-along, thought Agatha bleakly.

Sure enough. The words of "It's a Long Way to Tipperary" appeared on the screen. Why an old First World War song, wondered Agatha, and then came to the conclusion that they were possibly frightened that anything more modern would incur royalties. From previous experience, she knew that amateur dramatic companies seemed to think the eyes of the world were on them. It seemed to go on forever. He got the men to sing, then the women, then the children. "Follow the bouncing ball," he yelled, strutting about the stage in his moment of glory.

The curtains were drawn again and opened to reveal a cardboard cottage. The Babes were played by two ill-favoured children, who turned out to be the son and daughter of the head of the parish council, which was why they had landed the parts.

"Here comes the ogre again," said Mrs. Bloxby.

"Isn't there supposed to be a witch?" said Agatha.

"Shhh!" admonished a voice behind them.

"Fee! Fie! Fo! Fum! I smell the blood of an Englishman," roared Bert. "Be he alive,

10

or be he dead, I'll grind his bones to make my bread."

He was a burly man with a big round head and small glittering eyes, wearing built-up boots to make him look like a giant.

Slowly descending on a creaking wire came the Good Fairy. It broke when she was nearly down and she fell on a heap on the stage. "Can't you bloody bastards do anything properly?" she yelled. The children whistled and cheered.

"Shame!" called a voice from the audience. "Remember the children."

The Good Fairy rallied, picked up her bent wand and faced the ogre. "I am banishing you to the pit from whence you came," she said.

There was an impressive puff of green smoke. A trapdoor opened and Bert disappeared. The small orchestra started to play a jolly tune. A chorus lineup of ill-assorted tap dancers thudded their way across the stage. The pantomime dragged on to the close. At the final curtain, there was no sign of Bert.

"It was all right, considering it was an amateur show," ventured Mrs. Bloxby.

Agatha bit back the nasty remark that was rising to her lips. The two women had come in their separate cars. She said goodnight to her friend, warning her to drive carefully, because the fog was even thicker.

As Agatha was nearing Carsely, police cars heading for Winter Parva raced past on the other side of the road. Agatha did a U-turn and followed them. "Something's up," she muttered. "Maybe someone's murdered that dreadful comedian."

Soon she could see flashing blue lights outside the village hall.

The thick mist meant she was able to get into the car park before the police taped off the area. Where was the stage door? That chap, Gareth, had left and gone round the side of the building.

She walked round the side of the building and found a small door, standing open. A policeman supporting Gareth Craven came along a corridor inside. "If I could just get some fresh air," said Gareth. His face was chalk white.

Agatha stepped boldly forward. "I'm a friend of Mr. Craven," she said. "I'll look after him. You can come out when you're ready and take a statement. I have a Peugeot parked outside."

"Name?"

"Mrs. Bloxby," said Agatha, fearing that the sound of her own name would alert the policeman to the fact that she was a private detective.

"Registration number of your car?"

Agatha gave it to him and then put an arm around Gareth's waist. "Come along," she said. "I've some brandy in the car."

"I thought you were Agatha Raisin," said Gareth.

"I am," said Agatha, "but I didn't want that policeman to know that. Here we are. In you go and I'll get the heater on."

Once Gareth was settled in the passenger seat and had taken a few swigs of brandy from a flask Agatha kept in the car, Agatha said, "What happened in there?"

"It was awful," said Gareth. "When Bert didn't appear for the curtain call, I went back to look for him. He wasn't in any of the dressing rooms. I went down under the platform and there he was. Oh, God!"

He buried his face in his hands. Agatha waited until she thought he had recovered and said, "Go on. What happened to him?"

"He was standing there, very still, his mouth opened in a sort of awful silent scream. There was a big pool of blood at his feet. I couldn't find a pulse. I ran upstairs and phoned police, ambulance and fire brigade. The lot. I couldn't bear any more. That's it."

There was a peremptory rap on the car

window. Agatha lowered it and found Detective Sergeant Bill Wong staring accusingly at her. "I'll speak to you later," he said. "Mr. Craven. Please come with me. We need a statement. And Mrs. Raisin, please drive your car beyond the taped-off police area."

Bill must be really cross to call me Mrs. Raisin, thought Agatha. The young detective was the first friend she ever made when she came to the Cotswolds.

She decided to drive home and wait for the news the following day. Whatever had happened to Bert, it would be too late for the morning papers, but there might be something on television. But if it were an accident, then nothing would appear at all.

She was to get the news from an unexpected quarter.

The following day was Sunday. Agatha contemplated making one of her rare visits to morning service, thought better of it, turned over and went back to sleep.

She did not get up until midday. She rose, dressed and went down to feed her cats, Hodge and Boswell, and let them out into the garden. An icy wind was blowing. Both cats turned on the threshold and looked up at her.

"Go on," urged Agatha. "You've got fur

14

coats on, haven't you?"

Just then, the front doorbell rang. When Agatha opened the door, it was to find a tired-looking Mrs. Bloxby on the step.

"It's awful," said the vicar's wife.

"Come in," said Agatha. "I'll put the coffee on."

She waited until her friend was seated at the kitchen table with a mug of coffee, and asked, "What's going on?"

"I've been out a good part of last night. Mrs. Simple was in a terrible state. She asked to speak to Alf." Alf was the vicar. "We both went to Winter Parva. The doctor had been called and had given Mrs. Simple a tranquilliser but she was still in a state. She said God was punishing her for being a bad wife."

"Was Bert's death murder? Was she saying she killed him?" asked Agatha.

"No, not at all. But it appears to have been a particularly vicious murder. And well thought out, too. A small square had been cut out of the elevator platform. Evidently it always descended a bit too quickly and landed with a bump. Well, when Mr. Simple descended, a long steel spike had been embedded in the floor so that it went up through the hole in the platform, right between his legs and up into his body. Alf

15

and I managed to persuade Mrs. Simple to go to bed and we sat and talked quietly to her until she fell asleep."

"Doesn't Winter Parva have a vicar?"

"No, Alf takes services there twice a month."

"Wait a bit," said Agatha. "I don't get this. How on earth would anyone have time to fix that spike and not be discovered?"

"Mr. Simple was killed the first time he descended. That was towards the end of the pantomime. Evidently he had been complaining about the speed it went down and said he would only do it the once."

"But there would be a dress rehearsal!"

"I suppose so. His son, Walt, told us that no one goes down there except the black-smith."

"Do we have blacksmiths in this day and age?"

"Yes, of course. We have three hunts around here. And Mr. Crosswith, the black-smith, also does wrought-iron gates and things. Bert had been complaining that the trap was a bit dangerous. Mr. Crosswith designed a star trap from some old Victorian drawings."

"What is a star trap?" asked Agatha.

"Star traps consist of a permanent stage floor, made up of several triangular sections

16

of flooring meeting at the centre, which may be lifted but which naturally fall flat. Under the stage is an elevator using counterweights that are heavier than the weight of the performer.

"To make an impressive entrance, the elevator platform is first lowered, at which point a brake is applied, to stop the counterweight falling. The performer steps onto the platform. On cue, the brake is removed allowing the counterweights to fall. The performer is thrust through the star trapdoor. When the platform hits the highest point the performer leaps upward clearing the trapdoor sections, which then fall back into position at floor level. With a puff of smoke, the illusion is complete. Then in reverse, the flats open and Mr. Simple descends. Do you understand all that?"

"Sort of," said Agatha cautiously. "How do you know all this?"

"The Mothers' Union was given a tour of the hall earlier this year to show how it had been used back in the Victorian days. The blacksmith gave us a lecture on the trap."

"Do you think someone tampered with the brakes so that the platform would go down extra fast?"

"Maybe. But it went down pretty fast anyway."

"How does anyone get in under the stage? Is there an outside door?"

"You can get through under the platform at the front. I know that. But whether there is another entrance, I can't say. I know Bert only made one entrance through the trap, so it could have been tampered with any time earlier."

Agatha lit a cigarette and watched the smoke drift up towards the kitchen ceiling. "Wait a minute. In order for Bert to disappear, someone below the stage must have operated the elevator."

"I gather that the stage manager pressed a button at the side of the stage, which opened the trap and sent the green smoke up."

"But the stage manager — or Gareth Craven, the producer — surely checked on the apparatus before the show."

"If things went all right at the dress rehearsal, Mrs. Raisin, maybe a check wasn't considered necessary," said Mrs. Bloxby.

We really should start to call each other by our first names, thought Agatha. We called each other by our second names in the Ladies Society. But the society is long gone.

"What about the spike, or whatever it was

18

that killed Bert?"

"I don't know about that. Someone must have really hated him," said Mrs. Bloxby. "Such an elaborate way of killing him!"

"The blacksmith must be the obvious culprit," said Agatha.

"I believe he is a quiet, sensitive man," said Mrs. Bloxby.

"Oh, well," said Agatha. "I'll need to leave this one to the police. I've got my own business to run and I can't see anyone in Winter Parva wanting to pay me to investigate the murder of a baker."

On a Monday morning, a week later, Agatha, as usual, greeted her staff before settling down to have her usual breakfast at her desk — one cup of strong black coffee and two cigarettes. Her staff consisted of young, blond and beautiful Toni Gilmour; white-haired gentle Phil Marshall; lugubrious ex-policeman Patrick Mulligan; young Simon Black with his jester's face; and secretary, Mrs. Freedman. Simon had left briefly to work for another agency when he thought Toni had resigned. But when he heard Toni had returned, he had promptly asked for his job back. Agatha did not like Simon much, but had rehired him in a weak moment.

Agatha blew out a smoke ring. Mrs. Freedman gave an admonitory cough and switched on an extractor fan she had insisted on having installed.

"Let's see," said Agatha. "Toni and Simon, you have Mrs. Fairly's case. She wants proof of her husband's infidelity. Phil and Patrick, you've got two missing teenagers. You've got their details and photographs?"

Both nodded.

"Right," said Agatha. "I've got Berry's supermarket. Valuable goods have been disappearing from their electronics section and so far there's been nothing on their CCTV cameras. I'm going to spend the day there."

"Someone's coming," said Toni. "Might be something interesting." Toni hoped it might be a job that she could do on her own. She did not like working with Simon. He was constantly asking her out on dates and she found it all embarrassing.

The door opened and a man Agatha recognised as Gareth Craven walked in. He was even better looking than Agatha remembered. She did a frantic mental check. Did she have coffee-stained teeth? Had her lipstick faded? Why had she opted for trousers and flat shoes?

Gareth Craven was a tall man with thick

brown hair, clear grey eyes, a firm mouth, and a handsome face which unfortunately ended in a rather weak chin.

"Please take a seat, Mr. Craven," said Agatha, thinking, nobody's perfect.

"I really need your help," said Gareth. "You see, the newspapers are after me already and they are making me feel guilty. You would think I had done it. I've stopped answering the door or the phone. Mrs. Raisin, you have such a good reputation for solving cases. I wondered if I could employ you."

"Certainly," said Agatha. "Mrs. Freedman will draw up a contract for you. I will start on it right away. Toni, you take over Berry's supermarket for me." Simon's face fell. He had been looking forward to a day with Toni.

Mrs. Freedman came over with the contracts. Gareth barely looked at the price and quickly signed them.

"Now," said Agatha to Gareth, "we'll clear off somewhere for a coffee and you can give me all the details."

In the old-fashioned gloom of the George Hotel lounge, after coffee had been served, Agatha asked, "Who, in your opinion, would want to kill Bert?"

"That's the problem," said Gareth. "I

don't know where to tell you to start."

"Have you discussed it with your wife?" asked Agatha.

"I'm not married. Divorced."

"Like me," said Agatha cheerfully. "What about the blacksmith?"

"Harry Crosswith is a pillar of the community. He's in a terrible state."

"How could anyone guarantee that the spike would kill Bert? I mean, he could have been at the edge of the platform?"

"It's a small platform," said Gareth, "and Bert is — was — a big man. He complained that the lift went down too fast. In fact he and Harry had a bit of a row about it. Harry was very proud of that trap."

"What about the nearest and dearest. How old is the son, Walt?"

"He's twenty. Works in the bakery. Quiet and reliable."

"And Mrs. Simple?"

Gareth's face softened. "Gwen is a saint. She works serving in the shop. Everybody loves her."

Not you, I hope, thought Agatha. Aloud she said, "Perhaps I should start today by asking some of the locals. Who's the biggest gossip in the village?"

"Well, there's Marie Tench. But she can be spiteful."

"Maybe just the sort of person I should talk to," said Agatha. "Have you her address?"

"She's got a flat above the newspaper shop opposite the old marketplace."

"I'll start there. Tell me about yourself. How did you get involved with producing this pantomime?"

"I was a producer with BBC Radio 4 for years. Last year, I was suddenly made redundant. They're cutting jobs all round. It was a bit of a blow, but I'm lucky enough to have private means so I thought I would keep my hand in by producing this pantomime."

"But it wasn't very professional, surely," said Agatha. "I mean, it was a sort of mishmash of all the pantomime characters."

"I know. Mrs. Grant of the Women's Institute wrote the script and was to produce it, but she died. I wanted to make changes but the cast protested and said it should be kept just the way it was, in her memory."

"Any friction amongst the cast?"

He sighed. "I think amateur productions are worse than professional ones for fragile egos. The Good Fairy, Pixie Turner, went on as if she had a leading role in a Shakespeare production. Then that so-called comedian was always groping the chorus girls."

"Where does the chorus line come from?"

"Winter Parva High School. They have tap dancing classes there."

"Any little Lolitas that Bert might have had his eye on?"

"Oh, no! He was devoted to his wife."

"I think I've enough names to be going on with," said Agatha. "I'll start with the village gossip and then maybe later on you can introduce me to the blacksmith if the police aren't still grilling him."

Agatha drove to Winter Parva and parked in the main street. The village was a mixture of old houses with high, sloping roofs. Seventeenth-century buildings rubbed shoulders with Georgian and Tudor. The market hall, carefully preserved with its open arches and cobbled floor, was a fifteenth-century building. The village was situated down in a fold of the Cotswold hills. It was often misty. The River Oore ran under a bridge leading to the main street and this was blamed for the frequent fogs which plagued the place in winter. A pale sunlight was trying to permeate the mist as Agatha climbed the old stone stairs which led to Marie Tench's flat. Agatha rang the bell and waited. She had expected Marie Tench to be an old woman but the door was opened by a blonde with a quite enormous bust. She must have some sort of industrial-strength brassiere, thought Agatha, for the woman's breasts were hoisted up so far that it looked as if her head were peering over them.

"Mrs. Tench?" asked Agatha.

"It's Miss. Who are you?"

Agatha handed over her card and said, "Gareth Craven has asked me to investigate the murder of Bert Simple. He told me you knew a great deal about the village."

"Come in."

Agatha squeezed past her and found herself in a cluttered living room. Every surface was covered by some ornament. There were little glass animals along the mantelshelf, china figurines on the occasional tables, a collection of china coasters on the coffee table, and on a round table by the window, a large acid green vase of silk flowers.

Above the fireplace was a bad painting in oils of what appeared to be a naked Marie, those huge breasts painted in sulphur yellow and red.

Marie sat down on a chintz-covered sofa and waved one plump arm to an armchair, indicating that Agatha should be seated.

A shaft of sunlight shone through the window, lighting up Marie's face. Agatha reflected that Marie was wearing so much make-up, you could skate on it. She had a small prissy mouth painted violent red, a button of a nose, and cold grey eyes. Her hair was so firmly lacquered that it looked like a bad wig.

"I wondered if you had any idea who might have murdered Bert Simple," began Agatha.

"Pixie Turner, that's who."

"The Good Fairy?"

"Good Fairy, my arse. More like the wicked witch."

"But the murder of Bert Simple," said Agatha, "seemed to take a lot of knowledge of engineering and carpentry."

"Hah! Not much by all accounts. Any fool could have sawn that hole in the trap and shoved a spike underneath."

"How did you learn how the murder was done?"

"Molly Kite, her what works in the gift shop, told me. Her cousin's a policeman."

"Apart from Pixie, who else might have hated him enough?"

Did Marie suddenly look guilty — or was it a trick of the light? But she flashed Agatha a smile. "Apart from Pixie, we all loved Bert. No need to look anywhere else."

"And where does Pixie Turner live?"

"Out on the housing estate at the end of the village. I forget the number, but it's Church Road on the corner. Can't miss it. The door's painted bright blue."

Agatha drove to the housing estate. She saw the house with the blue door and parked outside. Suddenly, she felt inexplicably weary. Her friend, Mrs. Bloxby, could easily have diagnosed her trouble. Agatha Raisin, when she was not obsessed with some man or other, became de-energised. Sir Charles Fraith, with whom she had enjoyed an occasional fling, had disappeared out of her life as he did from time to time. Her ex-husband and next-door neighbour, James Lacey, was a travel writer and was currently abroad somewhere.

Agatha got slowly out of her car. She was wearing flat shoes and little make-up. Her brown hair was as glossy as ever but her bearlike eyes held a sad look. Her thoughts turned to Gareth Craven. Pity about that weak chin.

She squared her shoulders and marched up to Pixie's door and rang the bell.

The letter box opened and a voice cried,

"Go away!"

Agatha bent down. "I am Agatha Raisin and I am investigating the death of Bert Simple."

"Go away."

Agatha had a sudden inspiration. "I can understand you not wanting to be bothered. Those television crews will follow me around."

"Television!" The door swung open to reveal Pixie in a tatty pink silk dressing gown. "Come in quickly," she hissed, "and wait in the parlour until I get dressed."

Agatha looked around the room into which Pixie had thrust her. There were framed photographs of Pixie everywhere. Her acting roles appeared to have been confined to the village productions of pantomimes. She had progressed from Cinderella when she had been young, then to the Principal Boy, and so on to older parts, ending up as the Good Fairy.

A joss stick was smoking in a vase in one corner. Film and television magazines were piled up on the coffee table and on the chairs and sofa. One wall was dominated by a large mirror surrounded by light bulbs.

I wonder what she does when she's not dreaming of fame, thought Agatha.

Agatha peered at her own reflection in the

mirror. Was that a hair on her upper lip? "Snakes and bastards," she muttered, and began searching in her bag for a pair of tweezers. Not all that long ago, early fifties had been considered pretty old. Women let their figures sag and grew moustaches and didn't seem to bother. Ah, the good old days. She was still looking frantically for a pair of tweezers in her handbag when Pixie entered the room.

She had put on so much mascara that her lashes stuck straight out around her eyes like black spikes. She was wearing a short, tight red leather skirt with fishnet stockings and high heels. Her white blouse was nearly transparent. Her face had a sort of withered prettiness under white make-up with pink circles of blusher on each cheek. Her dyed blond hair was dressed in old-fashioned ringlets. She looked like a rather battered doll.

"Have the TV people called?" she asked anxiously.

Agatha was about to lie and say they would be along shortly in order to keep Pixie's interest when there was a ring at the doorbell.

"That'll be them," said Pixie and sashayed to the door.

Agatha heard a man's voice say, "Midlands

Television." Well, I'll be damned, she thought.

She walked into the small entrance hall to hear what Pixie was saying. "I was playing the part of the Good Fairy," said Pixie, "only don't let that fool you. Little Pixie can be wick-*ED*." Then she let out a great laugh which actually sounded like Har! Har! Har!

"Was there any friction amongst members of the cast?" asked the reporter.

"Oh, no. We got on great. Everyone loved Bert."

"Could anyone have got in under the stage to rig that murder device?"

"Yes, but take it from little Pixie here, it was some maniac from outside."

"Thank you for your time, Miz Turner."

"Don't you want to come in for a little drinkie?"

"No, got to get on."

Agatha retreated to the parlour. Pixie came in looking sulky and was about to sit down when the doorbell rang again.

"Maybe they're back," she said eagerly.

But this time, Agatha heard a voice say, *"Mircester Echo."*

Pixie tripped in followed by a reporter and cameraman. Agatha recognised the reporter, Chris Jenty.

"Why, Mrs. Raisin," he cried. "What a bit of luck."

"She's just leaving." Pixie's eyes bored into Agatha's face.

"How right you are," said Agatha with a smile. As she headed for the door, the reporter and cameraman followed her. "Come back!" wailed Pixie.

The slamming of her front door was the only answer.

"Let's go for a drink," said Chris. "You show me yours, and I'll show you mine."

When they were settled over drinks in a corner of the Jolly Beggar pub in the main street, Chris said, "You first."

Agatha told him what she had found out about the rigged trap, that the village gossip had suggested Pixie was the murderer, but that she hadn't got very far.

"Who's paying you to investigate this?" asked Chris.

"Can't tell you," said Agatha. "What have you got?"

"I've got a report of flaming rows between Bert Simple and Gareth Craven."

Agatha stared at him while her mind worked furiously. Once, before she had made a name for herself as a detective, she had been hired by a murderer who thought her incompetent and that the very act of

31

hiring her might make him look innocent.

"That's interesting," she said cautiously.

"All I can dig up at the moment. Have you seen Mrs. Simple?"

"I might try," said Agatha. "I hope she's not too sedated."

CHAPTER TWO

But when she left the pub, Agatha decided it was time she found out more about Gareth Craven. If he were retired, he must have private means or other work to be able to afford her fees.

She found his address and looked up his street on her iPad. It was quite close to the pub so she decided to walk. His home was in a narrow lane leading off the high street. It was in a terrace of seventeenth-century buildings that leant together as if trying to prop each other up. There were no gardens at the front of the houses.

As she raised her hand to ring the bell, she paused as a pleasant tenor voice sounded from inside the house, singing, "Take a Pair of Sparkling Eyes" from Gilbert and Sullivan's *The Gondoliers.*

Agatha waited until the end of the song and firmly rang the bell.

Gareth answered the door. He had a

charming smile, reflected Agatha.

"Was that you singing?" asked Agatha.

"Yes, I'm in amateur theatricals, for my sins."

Agatha's hormones gave a little sigh of disappointment. People who said "for my sins," in Agatha's opinion, had gnomes in the garden and avocado bathroom suites.

"Come in," said Gareth, standing aside to let her pass. "Turn left."

Agatha found herself in a small front parlour. Like Pixie, he had the walls and tables festooned with photographs of himself. She could understand people having family groups on display, but it did look like an excess of vanity to have so many pictures of oneself. Still, she reflected, maybe it was healthier than her own dislike of her appearance. She could remember, as a child, praying that she would wake up one morning with curly blond hair and green eyes.

"I belong to the Mircester Savoy Players," said Gareth. "You must come and see us. Sometimes I either sing or produce. I'm producing *The Mikado.*"

"Maybe another time," said Agatha. "Have you heard anything more that might be useful to me?"

"Not really. Of course there were a lot of squabbles amongst the cast. Like a professional company, we have our fair share of prima donnas."

"Who, for example?"

He furrowed his brow and then burst out laughing. "The lot of them, I think."

"So was the late Bert the cause of any of these squabbles?"

"Let me see. Pixie wanted the green smoke cancelled because she said it made her cough. Bert called her an old frump and she went into hysterics. Wait a bit! She shouted out something about did his wife know who he was screwing."

"To which he replied?"

" 'If I were married to a used-up bit of shit like you, I might think of being unfaithful to my wife. But I'm not so why don't you . . .' Well, you can guess the rest."

"Anyone else?"

"George Southern, the comedian, was going to take Bert to court. George put a whoopee cushion in the trap so that when Bert made his exit at one rehearsal there was the sound of a loud fart. He came roaring back up like the pantomime demon he's supposed to be and punched George on the nose. It was all soothed over."

"Dear me, so many suspects. I've lost my programme. Have you got a spare?"

"Right here." He handed her one.

"It's quite a small cast," said Agatha. "The principals, I mean. Mother Hubbard is someone called Bessie Burdock. There seemed to be no storyline at all. There was one scene where Mother Hubbard chases the school-children who did that tap dancing thing, in and out of a large cardboard shoe. Then Jack hands her some beans and she chases him as well. No beanstalk. Jack threatened by giant and saved by Puss in Boots played by Pixie. Double role?"

"Yes, she played Red Riding Hood as well."

"Blimey! Who played the wolf? Not mentioned here."

"The wolf changed his mind and said he would not be associated with such rubbish."

"And he is?"

"The English teacher at Mircester High School."

"And did he quarrel with Bert?"

"Yes. Told him the whole panto was an ego trip for Bert. If you remember, Bert makes an entrance and exit by the trap, but other times he simply walks on stage."

"And was that part of the nonexistent plot?"

"Well, no."

"But as the producer, surely you could have stopped him?"

"He said if I did, he would say I had been diddling one of the school kids. You know all the scandals at the BBC at the moment with everyone coming out of the woodwork to say they were sexually assaulted? Well, mud sticks. I couldn't risk it. I'll never produce another panto for them again."

"What happened to the last producer?"

"He died of a heart attack."

"I heard you had a flaming row with Bert," said Agatha cautiously. "Was that about the slander?"

"Yes."

"Didn't threaten to kill him or anything like that?"

"I did. So you see how terribly important it is for you to find the murderer."

"I'll do my best. Now, murders are usually committed by the nearest and dearest."

"You can forget that one," said Gareth, turning red. "Gwen Simple is a saint and the son, a quiet, well-mannered boy."

"You know the family well?"

"I knew Gwen before she was married. I would have proposed to her myself, but I was married at the time and Bert snapped her up."

No hope here, thought Agatha. He's obviously still carrying a torch for Gwen.

Aloud, she said, "I think it's time you

37

introduced me to the blacksmith."

"I'll get my coat."

The blacksmith was shoeing a horse. "We'd better wait until he's finished," said Gareth. "The work used to be done by a farrier, but he died a few years ago and Harry took on the extra work."

Agatha and Gareth sat on a couple of battered chairs in the workshop. Gates and railings, grills and pieces of wrought ironwork lay about them.

A thin wintry sun slanted through the open door where hens, sounding like rusty gates, pecked in the yard outside. Harry had trimmed the hoof and was attaching the horseshoe. I wonder what it would be like, thought Agatha, to work with one's hands and never have to exercise one's brain about who it was murdered whom.

"I'm amazed the horse is so patient," said Agatha.

"Doesn't hurt. Like getting your nails manicured," said Gareth.

At last the blacksmith had finished. "What is it?" he demanded.

Gareth introduced Agatha. Harry was a powerful man and loomed threateningly over Agatha.

"Look here," he said. "You find out who

murdered Bert and I'll shake that man's hand. The world's a better place without him."

"But what a horrible way to die!" protested Agatha.

"Aar, right up the goolies he got it. Serves him right. Got a decent wife. No reason to get his leg over half the village."

"Anyone in particular?" asked Agatha.

"I ain't one to spread the muck around now that bastard's dead. You're a detective, ain't you? Find out yourself."

A thin woman huddled in a shabby tweed coat came into the shed carrying a flask and a mug. "I brought your tea, Harry," she said.

"Put it down on the bench and get out o' here," he said.

She scuttled off, her head bent. I would like to get her alone, thought Agatha. She's been crying.

"Well, go on," roared the blacksmith.

"That's his work," said Agatha outside. "Where's his home?"

"It's a cottage round the back. I wouldn't go there if I were you. If Harry catches you, he'll be furious."

"Oh, come on," said Agatha impatiently.

"Actually, I've got a lot to do." Gareth hurried off, leaving Agatha glaring after him.

She squared her shoulders and went round the back of the shed.

The blacksmith's home was a plain red-brick building with a scarred front door that looked as if someone had periodically tried to kick their way in. The window frames were badly in need of painting.

The door was standing open. Agatha rapped on it and called out, "Anyone home?"

Mrs. Crosswith emerged from the dark nether regions of the house. She had discarded her coat and was wearing an apron made out of an old sack. From her straggly unkempt hair down to her old cracked shoes she looked like a photograph of rural poverty in the forties. Her faded face showed vestiges of what had once been a pretty woman. There was a purple bruise on one cheek.

Impulsively, Agatha asked, "Does your husband beat you?"

One red hand crept up to cover the bruise. "Only when he has had the drink taken," she said mournfully.

"Do you have children?" demanded Agatha.

"No."

"Then let's get you into a shelter for battered women. You don't need to put up with this treatment."

"You leave my Harry alone," she shrieked. "You come round here, interfering. Get yourself a man."

Agatha turned away in disgust. A clod of earth struck her on the back of the head. She swung round, picked up the clod and hurled it straight at the blacksmith's wife. It struck her full in the face.

Running back to her car, Agatha drove off as quickly as possible and then parked some distance away, switched off the engine and began to claw bits of earth from her hair.

There was a rap at the car window and Agatha shied nervously, expecting to see the furious face of the blacksmith. But it was Charles Fraith, smiling at her. Agatha lowered the window. "Have you been rolling on the ground with the local fellows?" he asked.

"No. I've just been assaulted by the blacksmith's wife. I need junk food. I'm going to the nearest McDonald's."

Charles went round the other side of her car and let himself into the passenger seat. "The nearest McDonald's is in Evesham," he said.

"Don't care," muttered Agatha, switching on the engine. "I'll tell you all about it when we get there."

"Rather like some sex," said Charles, wiping his fingers after disposing of a Big Mac. "Better in the anticipation than the reality."

Do you mean sex with me? Agatha wanted to ask, but feared the answer and started to talk about the little she knew about the case. A lump of earth she had missed fell out of her hair onto the table. An employee rushed forward with a damp cloth and cleared it up.

"So why did the blacksmith's wife throw a clod of earth at you?" asked Charles.

A shaft of sunlight came through the window and lit up his neat, composed features, barbered hair and tailored clothes.

"I think she's one of those martyrs," said Agatha bitterly. "I bet if I'd got her out of there and she got a divorce, the next thing you know, she'd be off with the same sort of man. She's eminently beatable. You know the type. They crave sympathy like a drug. I think the blacksmith did it. He was the one that put the trap in."

"The way you've described it," said Charles, "makes the whole village seem suspect. Why don't you get Toni to help you?"

Agatha fought down a pang of jealousy. "I suppose I could do with some assistance," she said. "I wonder whether I can get near the wife now."

"No time like the present," said Charles. "But I warn you. She is probably surrounded by helpful neighbours who won't let us near her."

When they drove away from Evesham, the sky had turned leaden grey. "Looks like snow," said Charles.

"Surely not," said Agatha. "What about global warming?"

"That's up at the North Pole. Nobody told the weather gods to lay off the Cotswolds."

Agatha drove along the main street of Winter Parva and then suddenly stopped with a screech of brakes. "What happened?" asked Charles.

"Look!" exclaimed Agatha. "The baker's shop is open."

"Probably some help."

"I'll park and have a look inside anyway," said Agatha. "Why can one never see a parking place in these villages?"

"There's one right there."

"You forget. I need a parking place the size of a truck."

"Let me at the wheel and I'll park for you."

The parking expertly effected, they both got out and walked into the shop. A tall, slim young man with a sensitive face was serving customers, aided by a small, chubby girl with rosy cheeks.

Agatha and Charles inched forward until they were at the counter. "Are you Walt Simple?" asked Agatha.

"Yes."

"My condolences on your sad loss."

"Want to buy anything?" he asked.

"I am a private detective, Agatha Raisin, employed by Gareth Craven to find the murderer of your father. Is it possible to have a word with your mother?"

"Mum's in the back shop, having a break." He lifted a flap on the counter. "Go through."

He led the way past gleaming ovens and into a small parlour where Gwen Simple sat, drinking tea.

The baker's wife looked as if she had stepped down from a mediaeval painting. She had blond hair worn in an old-fashioned chignon which gleamed in the soft light from a table lamp beside her. She had a dead-white face, a long thin nose and thick hooded lids, shielding brown eyes. Her wool dress of green and gold was long. Her hands were very white with long, tapered fingers.

"Mum," said Walt, "this is that detective woman. I've got to get back to the shop."

"May we sit down?" asked Agatha.

Gwen nodded.

"This is a colleague of mine, Charles Fraith. I am Agatha Raisin. We are so sorry for your loss. Have you any idea who might have done such a dreadful thing?"

"No. You must have tea. Wait."

Charles watched Gwen, fascinated, as the woman's white fingers put tea into a pot and added boiling water from a kettle steaming on the Aga cooker in the corner. Her movements seemed to flow. It was like watching a sort of tea-making ballet. When she had put the tea with cups and saucers on the plain wooden table along with milk and sugar, she went to the fridge and produced a plate of iced buns filled with fresh cream and strawberry jam.

"You must try this," she said in a gentle Gloucester accent. "The strawberry jam is my own."

Charles did not much like sweet things but he felt almost hypnotised into taking a bun.

"This is delicious," he said.

45

She smiled warmly at him, a small thin curved smile. "Mrs. Raisin?"

"No, thank you," said Agatha. "Got to watch my figure." Agatha's mind was working busily. There was no sense of mourning in this house.

"Do you miss your husband?" she asked bluntly.

Gwen raised pencil-thin eyebrows, suddenly making Agatha feel crude and clumsy.

"Of course," she said. "But it is all too horrible to take in, so Walt and I go on as usual. I will be glad when the body is released and we can mourn properly."

"Who would want to murder your husband?" asked Charles.

"I can't believe that anyone would," she said. "Everyone liked and respected Bert."

"But Mr. Crosswith said that your husband had affairs."

Those heavy lids masked her eyes for a moment. Then she looked steadily at Agatha. "Please leave. You are upsetting me. This is nothing more than malicious gossip."

"We are very sorry," said Charles. "But we must ask these awful questions."

"I do not want to speak to you anymore." She rose to her feet.

Charles took her hand. "If there is anything we can do . . ."

She smiled faintly. "I will let you know. But not her."

Charles handed Gwen his card and ushered Agatha out through the shop.

"Don't say anything until we get in the car," muttered Charles. "You look ready to explode."

"What a creepy phoney!" exclaimed Agatha, as soon as Charles was in the driving seat. "I bet she did it."

"How could she manage all the technicalities?" said Charles. "But I tell you one thing. La Belle Dame sans Merci is the sort of woman most men would kill for."

"La Bell . . . who?"

"It's a poem by John Keats about a knight who is seduced by a fairy."

"She's just an ordinary housewife," said Agatha jealously.

"Come on, Aggie. She looks as if she'd stepped down from a tapestry."

"Well, you must admit, Charles, the lack of mourning is most odd."

"Shock takes people strange ways."

"I do believe you're smitten."

Charles grinned. "You're jealous because she can make strawberry jam and bake while you just nuke stuff in the microwave."

"I think her son does the baking and that jam was probably made by a local. I don't believe a word that woman says."

"Don't worry, Agatha, I'll hear from her quite soon."

"Big-headed, aren't you?"

"Not at all. She will study my card and see the title. She will look me up on the Internet and find I am not married. She wants the best for her son. Oh, let's go and interview someone else. Look! Here comes the snow."

Tiny little flakes were spiralling upwards as the streetlights blossomed in the late-afternoon gloom. "I don't like it when the snow seems to be falling upwards," said Charles. "Must have got really cold."

"I'll phone Gareth and get the address of Bessie Burdock," said Agatha. "She played Mother Hubbard."

Bessie Burdock lived on the council estate, which was, like all council estates, on the edge of the village. Most of the council houses were now privately owned. They were trim, stone, two-storied buildings with well-kept gardens, or what looked like well-kept gardens under the increasing blanket of snow.

Bessie, a voluminous woman, answered

the door. From behind her came the sounds of screaming children. Agatha explained who they were and what they wanted.

"Come in," she said. "I'll get my daughter, Effie, to shut this lot up. Effie! Get 'em out into the back garden and make a snowman."

A heavily tattooed teenager in a Goth outfit said, "Right, Mum. But I'm sick o' the bastards."

Bessie led them into a cosy front room. "Are all those children I hear yours?" asked Agatha.

"No, thank goodness," said Bessie. "I mind the kids until their parents get back from work."

Agatha thought she even looked the part of Mother Hubbard. Bessie was very fat. She had a big round head and several chins and a huge bosom.

"You'll want to know about Bert," she said. "Right awful to die that way. Must be some madman."

"Did you like him?" asked Charles.

"No, I didn't. I was sorry for Gwen, his wife. He was a crude bully. Great baker, mind you. Folks come from miles around to buy stuff at the village bakery."

"Did he have affairs?" asked Agatha.

"Gossip here and there. That's all. Nobody ever had any proof. My Effie loathed him."

"Why? Did he make a pass at her?"

"No. He'd just shout insults at her in the high street, called her Night of the Living Dead. This Goth thing is just a phase. Folks are saying Gareth Craven maybe did it."

"Why?" asked Charles and Agatha in unison.

"Gareth always fancied Gwen. He wanted to marry her at one time. When she got married to Bert, he went off and married someone else and that didn't work out."

"Who was Gareth married to?"

"Some woman in the BBC. She didn't like it here. When they were married, Gareth lived in London. He kept on his house and came back here after he got the sack. That's why he joined that Gilbert and Sullivan lot in Mircester. Gwen's one of the stars."

"If Bert Simple was the bully I believe him to have been," said Agatha, "I'm surprised he allowed her to be part of it."

"I think he was proud of her. There were always plenty of local girls to work in the bakery behind the counter."

"Any of the girls report any trouble?"

"No. A lot fancy Walt."

"I'm surprised the bakery is still open," said Agatha.

"Walt told people that he and his mum found it the best way to cope with grief.

50

They said Bert would have wanted it that way."

Agatha asked more questions, not so much in the hope of gaining anything new, but of a reluctance to leave the cosy, chintzy room and go back out into the cold snow.

At last they thanked her and took their leave.

"Now for the First Murderer," said Charles.

"And who's that?" asked Agatha.

"Why, Gareth Craven. Who else?"

CHAPTER THREE

Charles noticed that Agatha insisted on repairing her make-up before approaching Gareth Craven's house.

His fears that Agatha might be in the grip of one of her unfortunate obsessions died when he met Gareth. The man was handsome, but in rather a weak way.

"I'm glad to see you," said Gareth. "Oh, the police are looking for you, Mrs. Raisin."

"Agatha, please. Why?"

"They came back to interview me again. They said that Mrs. Crosswith claimed you assaulted her."

"She threw a clod of earth at me and I threw it back," said Agatha.

"Well, they're just setting up a mobile unit next to the market hall," said Gareth. "Maybe you should drop in there and clear the matter up."

"All right," said Agatha irritably. "Why did the police want to see you again?"

"Oh, all that old history of me wanting to marry Gwen. If her husband had thought there was anything going on, he wouldn't have let her perform for me."

"Perform?" asked Agatha. "Do you mean he wanted to watch while you had sex with his wife?"

"Get your mind out of the sewer," snapped Gareth, turning red. "Gwen is the leading lady in the Mircester Players. We are going to put on a production of *The Mikado.* John Hale plays the Mikado's son and Gwen plays Yum-Yum. Gwen phoned me and said she wished to carry on with rehearsals. She is such a trouper. The police say the body will be released shortly. Everyone will feel better once the funeral is over."

"Where is the funeral to take place?" asked Charles.

"It's to be a non-religious service at Mircester crematorium."

"I don't know how everyone can feel better with a murderer at large," said Agatha. "Is anyone else carrying a torch for Gwen?"

"Any more remarks like that and I shall regret employing you, Agatha. If you mean, was anyone so much in love with her that they would kill her husband — no."

Except you, thought Agatha.

■ ■ ■ ■

They were just getting back into the car when Charles's mobile rang. Agatha heard him say soothingly, "I'll be right along."

Agatha looked at the rather smug smile on Charles's face. "Who was that?"

"The merry widow. She wants to talk to me."

"Good! Let's get going."

"I have been ordered to leave you behind."

"Snakes and bastards," howled Agatha. "Who's the detective? You or me."

"You, detective. Me, marriageable man. Geddit?"

"Got it," said Agatha sourly. "I may as well report to the police."

Agatha drove the short distance to the mobile police unit. She reflected that she was falling into the villager's lazy way of driving everywhere instead of walking.

To her relief, Bill Wong was there with two constables.

"I gather you've had a complaint about me," said Agatha.

"Yes, pull up a chair, Agatha. What happened?"

"I had spoken to her and was just leaving

when she threw a clod of earth that hit me on the head." Agatha bent her head over the desk and combed her hair with her fingers. Several little bits of earth fell onto the white pages of a report. "See? So I threw it back."

"Here's paper and pen. Write down what happened. I don't think we'll be taking it further. We have been called out several times in the past by Mrs. Crosswith, claiming her husband had attacked her, but she always backed down."

Agatha wrote busily and passed the report over to Bill.

"It's all getting more and more complicated," said Agatha. "It's always the same. Someone dies or gets murdered and, at first, everyone says what a great person the deceased was and then nasty things begin to seep out. What do you think of Mrs. Simple?"

"Seems an ordinary sort of housewife to me."

"Oh, Bill. I do love you."

"Then don't get under our feet," warned Bill. "I don't want you messing up a police investigation."

"Did I ever?"

"Often."

"And the result was, you got your murderer," said Agatha.

"And the result on one or more occasions was that the police had to rescue you," said Bill. "Off you go, and don't hide evidence."

Outside the mobile unit, Agatha phoned Charles, but his phone was switched off. She fought down a pang of jealousy. She remembered Gareth talking about the English teacher. Perhaps he might have some interesting views. She sent Charles a text message, got in her car and drove to Mircester High School. Pupils were streaming out through the gates, throwing snowballs, wrecking their school uniforms as they went along, the boys pulling their shirts out of their trousers and taking off their ties and the girls hitching up their skirts to above the knee.

Agatha parked her car and walked into the school, breathing in the smell of sweat, chalk and disinfectant. She stopped a female member of staff and asked where she could find the English teacher.

"Which one?" demanded the harried-looking woman.

"The one that sings in the opera."

"That'll be John Hale. I think I saw him in his classroom. Number 10b, along on your left, round the corridor."

Agatha walked on until she found the classroom. She put her hand on the door-knob and looked through one of the four glass windows on the upper part of the door.

John Hale was sitting at a desk, correcting papers.

He was beautiful. He had thick black glossy hair shadowing a pale sensitive face and perfect straight nose and mouth. Agatha quickly retreated and took out a compact, powdered her nose and repaired her lipstick.

She then opened the classroom door and walked in. "Can I help you?" he asked.

Yes, was the answer to that, thought Agatha. Throw me on the pommel of your white horse and ride off with me into the sunset. She handed him her card. "I am a private detective, investigating the death of Bert Simple."

He turned her card over with long sensitive fingers. No wedding ring, noticed Agatha.

"I don't know how I can help you," he said.

"It's like this," said Agatha. "The more I learn about Bert Simple, the better chance I have of finding out who murdered him." She saw a chair next to his and went and sat in it.

"He was a bully. How that saint of a wife of his put up with him is beyond me."

Sod his wife, thought Agatha, gripped by a pang of jealousy.

"You refused a part in the pantomime."

"The whole thing was a farce," said John. "Bert ran the show. He didn't care that there was no attempt at a plot so long as he could strut about the stage. But out of all the people in the cast, I cannot think of anyone who would go so far as to murder him. Amateur companies are full of scenes and rivalries but it doesn't mean anything. They think by stamping around that they are behaving like real pros. There was one thing, however."

"What was that?"

"The tap dancers from this school. There is a girl called Kimberley Buxton. It cropped up at the beginning of rehearsals. She said that Bert had given her a lift home and on the way had stopped the car and tried to assault her. Her parents reported the matter to the school."

"Not the police?"

"No. The matter was investigated. Kimberley backed down and claimed it was nothing. She had misunderstood the situation."

"And do you think she had?" asked Aga-

58

tha.

"We occasionally have trouble here with pupils trying to get back at the teachers with claims of sexual harassment. That is why we were relieved the police had not been contacted."

"How old is this girl?"

"She's fourteen now. She was thirteen at the time."

"I would like to speak to her," said Agatha.

"I don't think that's a good idea. I would like to help you." He smiled and Agatha blinked at the beauty of that smile.

"Okay," she said reluctantly. "You seem a very observant man, Mr. Hale."

"John, please."

"John it is. Perhaps I could take you for lunch and you could give me a picture of some of the people in Winter Parva."

He hesitated, while Agatha mentally crossed her fingers.

"I suppose that would be nice," he said slowly. "I've never met a private detective before."

"What about lunch on Wednesday at the George in Mircester? Be my guest."

"Yes, I think that would be all right. I'll phone you if I can't make it. What time?"

"Say one o'clock?"

"Right. Thank you."

Agatha left the school with a smile on her face. She was just getting into her car when Charles drove up.

"How did you get on?" asked Agatha.

"She seems to be finally mourning. She wept on my shoulder for quite some time. Apart from that, nothing interesting."

"Dear Gwen is manipulating you," said Agatha. "I'll bet she's glad to get rid of the beast."

"You get anything?" asked Charles.

"Only a bit of possible gossip." She told Charles about Kimberley. "He wouldn't give me the address but we'll look up Buxton in the phone book."

"Actually, I'm going to shove off. Why don't you get Toni along to help you?"

But Agatha did not want her beautiful detective anywhere near Winter Parva. Her head was already full of dreams of John Hale. Normally, Agatha's powerful sex drive would already have plunged her into obsession, but John's beauty had roused an almost teenage romanticism.

Charles walked to his car and then turned back. "What did this teacher look like?"

"What has that got to do with anything? Oh, tweedy. You know the type."

Charles threw her a suspicious look before getting into his car and driving off.

Fine snow was still falling. Evening was settling down with smells of tea and fried fish. One more interview, thought Agatha, and then I'd better get home before I am snowed up. She decided to leave Kimberley for another day and interview the comedian, George Southern. A small girl who looked anorexic was painting her nails behind the counter in the gift shop. Molly Kite, thought Agatha. The shop was filled with the usual Cotswold tourist junk: coffee mugs, tea towels, Cotswold fudge and other items meant to tempt the bus tours which came in the summer.

"I would like to speak to Mr. Southern," said Agatha.

Large black eyes framed in thick false eyelashes stared at her. "Oh, you'll be that detective lady. Have you got a gun?"

"No."

Molly promptly lost interest. "I'll fetch him."

She went through to the back shop. Agatha could hear the murmur of voices.

Then Molly reappeared. She whispered, "He won't see you. Says he's stock taking. That's a clue!"

"It is."

"Looked ever so shifty, he did. And he hated Bert."

"Why?"

"Cos Bert was real hateful."

"In what way?"

"The panto was Bert's big moment, see? He was jealous of his wife being the singing star o' Mircester. Said he could act her off the stage *and* that wimp, John Hale."

Diverted, Agatha asked, "And is John Hale a wimp?"

"Naw. He's a judo expert. One o' the big boys tried to take him on and Mr. Hale laid him flat on his back."

Agatha felt a twinge of unease. She hoped John hadn't fallen for Gwen. They must spend a lot of time together at the Mircester Players.

"Tell Mr. Southern I'll call again," said Agatha.

She walked out of the shop and stood outside. After she had counted to ten, she walked in again in time to hear him say, "Get rid of her all right?"

"Why, Mr. Southern," cooed Agatha. "I thought I heard your voice."

"Oh, what is it?" he demanded. "I want to get home before the roads are blocked."

"Did you murder Bert Simple?"

"Get the hell out of here and never speak to me again," roared George.

"I was just . . . ," began Agatha, and then ducked as a mug bearing the legend WEL-COME TO WINTER PARVA went sailing over her head. She beat a hasty retreat.

Agatha decided to go home to Carsely to look after her cats. It was a slow, treacherous journey. What if it's worse on Wednesday? fretted Agatha. What if I can't meet him for lunch?

She let herself into her thatched cottage. Her cats, Hodge and Boswell, wound their sinuous bodies round her ankles, nearly tripping her up. She prepared their meal of fresh fish and then cooked a microwavable vindaloo curry for herself.

When she had finished eating, Agatha phoned Toni and asked how the various investigations were going on.

"I might have a bit of gossip for you," said Toni. "A friend of mine was telling me that the widow, Gwen Simple, is the star of the Mircester Players, along with a school-teacher called John Hale. There are rumours of a romance there. Would you like me to pop round to the theatre and see if I can find out more?"

"No!" shouted Agatha. She could not bear the idea of beautiful Toni even breathing the same air as John. "I mean, you've got a lot to do. Get on with it and leave the Winter Parva case to me."

When Toni rang off, Simon, who was about to leave the office, said, "What's up with Aggie? I could hear her shouting no, right across the room."

"I think she might be in love again."

"Who with?"

"Never mind."

"Coming for a drink?"

"I've got a date," lied Toni.

Simon went out, slamming the door behind him. Toni sighed. If only Simon would find a girlfriend and stop pestering her.

The Cotswolds lay under a pristine coating of snow when Agatha set out the next day, hoping her snow tyres would grip the road. A white disk of a sun shone overhead. Scenes straight out of a Christmas card lay round every corner. Agatha marvelled at how innocent everything seemed. And yet someone had been driven to murder Bert Simple in an extremely brutal way.

Perhaps it was all to do with amateur dramatics and the fact that everyone wanted to be famous these days. That might cause murderous spite and a desire for revenge.

A man was walking his dog, children were

building a snowman in a garden — the school must be closed — and a woman was hurrying home with a basket of shopping. Agatha suddenly felt weary of detective work. People needed to be interviewed again. She had a sudden longing to stop the car and go up to a cottage and ask to sit by the fire and forget about the whole blasted business.

Then she thought that perhaps she should make a U-turn, go to the vicarage and use her friend, Mrs. Bloxby, as a sounding board. She slowly eased the car round on the icy road and headed back into Carsely.

Ten minutes later, Agatha was ensconced in the vicarage drawing room in front of a log fire with a cup of tea in one hand and a buttered scone in the other.

Mrs. Bloxby sat quietly with her hands folded in her lap, listening intently. When Agatha had finished, she said, "It seems to be a crime caused by sex and jealousy. If the murder had been performed in a murderous rage, it would be different. But someone plotted not only to kill him but to destroy his manhood in the process. Mrs. Simple is a very attractive woman."

"If you like that sort of thing," said Agatha sourly.

"Men do like that sort of thing. She has the looks to rouse protective feelings in men and also romanticism."

Don't say it, thought Agatha.

But Mrs. Bloxby went on. "Mrs. Simple is a leading light of the Mircester Players. They specialise in productions of Gilbert and Sullivan. The leading man, John Hale, is handsome, and the exact opposite of her husband. Have you thought of him?"

Most of the time, was the honest answer to that question, but Agatha said airily, "Oh, I've spoken to him. Too quiet and gentle."

Oh, dear, thought Mrs. Bloxby, studying her friend's face. I do believe Mrs. Raisin has fallen in love again.

"He is a karate expert," said Mrs. Bloxby.

Agatha shifted restlessly in her armchair. "Yes, yes. But he didn't throw Bert over his shoulder or break his neck. I think the blacksmith is the most likely candidate at the moment. He's violent, he beats his wife and he hated Bert. Also he is the one who knew all the mechanics of the trap."

"Then could a woman have done it?" asked Mrs. Bloxby. "On the face of it, it looks like a man's job. But it takes very little effort to sink a sharp pointed steel rod into concrete and saw a hole in the trap. You remember, he didn't enter the stage by the trap. He only left it. So someone had a lot of time to arrange things between the dress rehearsal the day before and the actual performance."

"That's right," said Agatha slowly.

"And there is a door at the side that leads directly under the stage."

"I didn't know that," said Agatha crossly. "I should have known."

"I didn't know until Mrs. Jelly who comes to our church told me. I knew you could get in from the front but I didn't know about the other door."

Agatha let out a groan. "My list of suspects suddenly seems to have got longer. I'd better get over there and get to work."

But Agatha was halfway to Winter Parva when she realised the following day was Wednesday and her date with John. She stopped the car abruptly and peered in the driving mirror. There were a couple of small wrinkles on her upper lip and two grey hairs on the crown of her head.

"Sod this detective business," she muttered. She phoned Phil Marshall on her mobile and asked him to meet her by the market hall in Winter Parva.

When Phil arrived, Agatha gave him her iPad with all her notes and told him to re-interview as many of the suspects as he could. She hoped that Phil with his white hair and gentle manner might get more out of people than she had done herself.

"And what will you be doing?" asked Phil.

"I've got a lead I'm following up," said Agatha. "I'll let you know if anything comes of it. There's a schoolgirl, Kimberley Buxton, who claims she was assaulted by Bert Simple. See if you can find out where she lives and get something out of her."

She then headed off for Evesham, planning a long day of restoration. First, she got a nonsurgical facelift at Beau Monde and then headed for her hairdresser, Cheryl at Achille, to get her hair tinted.

Evesham does not specialise in luxury goods and Boots did not have her favourite perfume, but she thought she had enough Mademoiselle Coco left at home. When she finally walked to the car park in Evesham, the weather had changed and a thaw had settled in. I hope this doesn't mean flooding, fretted Agatha. What if the River Mir floods again and Mircester is cut off?

That night, she tossed and turned, hearing snow falling from the thatched roof above her head.

In the morning, she laid out her clothes for

the day: a royal blue wool tailored jacket with a matching short skirt and high black suede boots. Over it, she planned to wear a white fun fur. She had her usual breakfast of one cup of black coffee and two Benson cigarettes before working on her make-up.

Still worried about floods, she left early, having some difficulty in driving because the heels on her boots were very high. The roads weren't too bad and so she arrived at the George Hotel car park exactly one hour too early. She fought off the temptation to go into the bar and have a couple of stiff gin and tonics.

How the minutes dragged! How incredibly boring were the programmes on the radio! She finally switched to Radio 3 in time to hear the announcer say, "And now we have a little-known symphony by Hans Guttenberger." Agatha switched it off, muttering, "The reason it's little known, you pompous pratt, is because nobody wanted to hear it."

At long last, the dial of her watch showed five minutes to one. She got out of her car and began to tittup across the melted snow of the car park on her high heels. Her foot slipped and she skidded forward and ended up under a parked car with her head poking out.

"Engine trouble?" asked a small man looking down at her. "Can I help?"

"Help me out of here," wailed Agatha. "I slipped."

He bent down, and grunting and groaning, pulled her out. Agatha staggered to her feet. Her white coat was ruined. She thanked her rescuer, stormed into the George, demanded to see the manager, and berated him about failing to salt the car park.

She was in full intimidating voice when suddenly she saw John walking into the hotel. "You'll hear from me later," she said to the manager, and turning, greeted John.

"I'll leave this mess of a coat in the cloakroom. I slipped and fell," said Agatha.

"Poor you. Are you all right?"

"Yes, I'm fine. I'll meet you in the bar."

Agatha went to the bar as quickly as her boots would allow and asked for a double gin and tonic and downed it in almost one gulp, feeling the blessed alcohol coursing through her veins.

John appeared at her elbow. He was wearing a well-tailored suit, a striped shirt and a blue silk tie which matched his eyes. "What'll you have?" asked Agatha.

"What's that you've got there?"

"Just tonic," lied Agatha. "But I could do

with something stronger. What about you?"

"Just a half of lager."

Agatha ordered another gin and tonic for herself and the lager for John. Then to her horror, John said, "I'll pay for these."

"No! You're my guest," said Agatha, but the barman had handed John the bill.

John insisted on paying. "We'll take our drinks to the table," said Agatha.

Why did I ever think I could wear these wretched boots? she mourned. And now he'll think I'm a lush.

When they were seated in the dining room, Agatha said, "I lied about that first drink because I felt I needed one after that silly fall in the car park. I didn't want you to think I was a drunk."

"No, I wouldn't think that." He smiled into her eyes. "Your skin is too perfect. I brought you along a couple of tickets for *The Mikado.* Monday is the opening night and we're having a party afterwards."

"I would love to come," said Agatha, her eyes shining.

He asked her about her work and Agatha was happy to talk, trying not to tell highly embroidered stories and failing as usual. She suddenly realised she had been monopolising the conversation and asked him why he became a schoolteacher.

"You think it's a boring job?" he asked.

"I think these days the life of any school-teacher is fraught with danger," said Agatha. "So why school teaching?"

"I am one of the last of the Mr. Chips," he said. "If I can inspire just one pupil to go on to university, then it is worth anything."

"I think you could inspire anyone," said Agatha.

"Are you flirting with me?"

"Maybe."

"I rather like that. We should have fun at the party."

Agatha dragged her soaring mind back to earth. "Have you no idea who might have murdered Bert?"

"Not a one. He was generally disliked. But murder! Can't think of anyone vicious enough. I'm happy for Gwen. She says she loved her husband, but how can she love anyone like that?"

"But she is performing in *The Mikado.*"

"Gwen is a real trouper."

Agatha experienced a sharp stab of jealousy. She said sharply, "Oh, come on. It's only an amateur show, not Covent Garden, and her husband isn't buried yet."

Those blue eyes of his suddenly looked as hard as sapphires. "I don't expect someone

72

like you to understand."

Agatha backpedalled like mad. "Of course, she will want to do anything to keep her mind off it," she said. "The show must go on."

He flashed that smile of his that made her feel as if her bones were melting. "There you are! I should have known you would really understand."

He glanced at his watch and gave an exclamation. "I am so sorry. I have a rehearsal. Got to run."

"I'll settle this," said Agatha. "See you on Monday."

After she had gone, she found to her delight that the meal was free, compliments of the hotel to make up for the unsalted car park and they had had her fun fur express cleaned.

She took off her boots and dug a pair of flat shoes out of the glove compartment, putting them on with a sigh of relief.

Now, what on earth am I going to wear on Monday? thought Agatha.

CHAPTER FOUR

By Sunday evening Agatha's bedroom was a mess. Clothes lay strewn everywhere. She glared sourly at her fun fur. Why call the damn thing "fun" when she would feel better off in mink. Why were the animal libbers so much against mink when the ferrety little creatures were roaming about destroying the native fauna of Britain?

Monday came. Agatha called in at the office to make sure all the cases were being covered. She sat down and studied the report from Phil. He had achieved a long interview with Gwen Simple. Gwen had denied that her husband was a philanderer. She had gone on at length about how much she would miss him. Then Agatha's eyes sharpened. Clever Phil had run Kimberley to earth. But interviewed with her parents, she denied having accused Bert Simple of having tried to molest her. She claimed it was only a joke which had turned out badly.

"I don't believe a word of it," muttered Agatha.

He had also interviewed the blacksmith, Pixie Turner and George Southern. The interview with George Southern was the one that had been singularly unsuccessful. In fact, Southern had threatened to call the police, saying he was a victim of harassment. Phil's comment was, "Southern is frightened. He knows something."

Agatha had still to find someone to take with her to *The Mikado.* She had considered Mrs. Bloxby. But she did not want her clever friend to find out about her interest in John Hale. Toni interrupted her thoughts. "I'm free at the moment. Would you like me to take a look at Winter Parva?"

Agatha surveyed her beautiful assistant. Her conscience troubled her. Toni was a brilliant detective but she wanted to keep the girl clear of John Hale. On the other hand, the case needed to be solved.

"Maybe one thing," said Agatha. "There's a schoolgirl called Kimberley Buxton. She claimed to have been assaulted by Bert Simple and now denies the whole thing. You're nearer her in age. See if you can get her to confide in you. Don't go to the school! Wait until she is home or on the way home." She unclipped a photograph. "Phil snatched this shot of her."

"Anything this morning?" asked Toni.

"I'll give you these notes. There's something fishy about George Southern. See if you can get anything out of him."

"Are you going over there yourself?"

"I think I'll sit here. Take a copy of the notes. I'll study them and see if I can think of anything. Where's Simon?"

"That divorce case."

"And Patrick?"

"The supermarket job."

"Okay. You run along."

But Agatha did not study the notes. She fretted over what to wear. The day was cold and frosty. Her mind ranged back and forwards over the clothes in her wardrobe. Of course, she could go to Bicester where they had model gowns at knock-down prices. But that would mean neglecting the case. Sod the case, thought Agatha, putting on her coat.

She bumped into Phil in the doorway. "Going to see someone," she said. "Are you doing anything this evening?"

"No. Why?"

"I've got a spare ticket for *The Mikado.* There's a party afterwards."

"That would be nice."

"I'll pick you up at seven thirty."

I mean old Phil doesn't look as if I could be romantically interested in him, thought Agatha cheerfully. He's old.

She had slight misgivings when she picked up Phil that evening. He was in full black-tie gear and his silver hair was brushed until it shone. I wish he looked a bit dowdier, thought Agatha. She was wearing a gold dress decked with little gold beads.

There seemed to be some delay to the opening of the operetta. Then Gareth Craven, introducing himself as the producer, appeared in front of the curtains. "Ladies and gentlemen," he said. "Unfortunately John Hale will not be appearing tonight. He has a bad cold. His place will be taken by George Southern."

"Oh, no!" said Agatha. "He's horrible. Let's go."

"Agatha," said Phil firmly, "we have a good chance to study the members of the cast, particularly Gwen Simple. I feel it would be a good idea to watch the show."

"Okay," said Agatha gloomily, banishing romantic dreams of serving John hot soup in front of a log fire.

The show began. With a wig and heavy make-up on, George Southern was just about passable as Nanki-poo. He sang, "A

Wand' ring Minstrel I," in a pleasant tenor, quite unlike the voice he had used to roar out the songs at the pantomime.

Agatha hoped to escape outside for a cigarette at the interval, but the audience was warned that there was only to be a break of two minutes.

The second act opened with the Three Little Maids. Gwen Simple sang "The Sun Whose Rays Are All Ablaze" in what even Agatha had to admit was a perfect soprano.

Then she leaned forward in her seat. Dominating the stage was a large box, covered in fancy paper and tied up with tinsel ribbon. The maids kept eyeing it. There seemed to be some sort of holdup backstage. "It's a present for me," said Gwen. Obviously improvising, she knelt down and unwrapped the box and threw the lid open.

Gwen let out one long scream, put her hands to her face and fainted dead away as the curtains were hurriedly closed.

"Come on, Phil," said Agatha. "We'd better get backstage." As they made their way out of the theatre, they could hear Gareth Craven telling the audience there had been an accident and to collect their money from the box office.

Fortunately, the stage door man was not at his post. They hurried along the corridors to the sound of screams and yells, stopping short in the wings.

On the brightly lit stage, Gwen was being supported by her "maids" at the side. A crowd of people were clustered around the box. Agatha thrust her way to the front and stared down at the contents. The severed head of George Southern stared up at her from the bloodsoaked interior of the box.

Agatha saw she was next to Gareth Craven. "Where's the rest of him?" she asked.

"In his dressing room, I suppose," said Gareth through white lips.

Inspector Wilkes strode onto the stage, followed by three detectives, one of whom was Agatha's friend, Bill Wong.

"Clear the stage," he shouted. "Is there a green room?"

"Yes," said Gareth.

"Get everyone along there and nobody leaves until the police have taken statements." He glared at Agatha. "And that goes for you, too."

He summoned two policemen who were waiting in the wings. "Make sure everyone

79

is in the green room and no one is to leave."

The green room was laid out for the after-show party. Efficient Phil commandeered two chairs for them and went to fetch Agatha a drink.

Everyone was white faced. Gwen had started to cry. Phil returned with a large gin and tonic. Agatha took a gulp. She saw Gareth looking at her and summoned him.

"Who played the Lord High Executioner? I seem to have lost my programme."

"Colin Blain."

The door to the green room crashed open. Inspector Wilkes surveyed the crowded room, his face a mask of contempt.

"Where is Mr. Southern?" he shouted.

"He's dead!" wailed someone.

"That head is a fake," said Wilkes bitterly. "Someone's idea of a practical joke."

Over the buzz of relieved voices, Agatha stood up and shouted, "You'll probably find him at home."

"And what gives you that idea, Mrs. Raisin?"

"He's a comedian. It was probably his idea of a joke."

"You can all go home," said Wilkes.

"Come on," said Agatha to Phil. "Let's get to Winter Parva."

"Where does he live?" asked Phil as Agatha roared out of Mircester.

"Maybe above the gift shop but all we have to do is look for all the flashing blue lights."

"What can they charge him with?"

"Wasting police time for a start," said Agatha.

The village of Winter Parva was in a hollow and thick mist had descended. As Agatha turned into the high street, she could see flashing blue lights outside the gift shop.

She parked the car. She and Phil got out and stood near the entrance to the gift shop. Two policemen appeared, escorting George to a police car. George was shouting, "It was only a joke."

"He must be mad," said Phil.

"There's a thought," said Agatha. "Mad people commit murders."

She dropped Phil off at his home and then drove to her cottage. Agatha still felt shaken and wondered if any of the cast would sue George for the distress he had caused. Gareth would probably try to get all the money back he had lost on refunded ticket sales.

Her doorbell rang. First, she peered cautiously through the spy hole. The vision that was John Hale stood outside, wreathed in mist.

Agatha wrenched open the door. "I just heard the awful news," said John.

"Come in. Let me take your coat. Let's have a drink and I'll tell you all about it. How did you hear what happened?"

"Gwen called me but she was too distressed to go on."

Agatha struck a match and lit the log fire which her excellent cleaner had laid ready. "Now, what would you like to drink?"

"Brandy, if you've got it."

Agatha poured two glasses, handed him one and sat down in an armchair. John was leaning back against the cushions of the sofa, very much at his ease.

After describing the shock the fake head had caused, Agatha surveyed John.

"I don't think you've got a cold," she said. "Why did you let George Southern take your place?"

"He begged me. He said it was a dream of his to have the leading role. He's got a good voice and I thought one evening wouldn't hurt."

"The police will be looking for you," said Agatha. "If they think you both planned it, you will be charged along with George."

"I had no idea the silly fool planned such a horrible joke. Oh, dear. Poor, poor Gwen. She must be in bits."

You can go off people, you know, thought Agatha. Yes, he's beautiful. But what if I'm sitting here with a murderer?

She said, "Perhaps you had better go home. The police will be looking for you."

"I suppose I must." He got to his feet.

The doorbell rang shrilly, startling both of them. Agatha went to answer it, peering through the spy hole and seeing Bill Wong standing on the step. "Come in," she said, opening the door. "There's someone here you'll want to interview."

"I wanted to talk to you and ask you what you were doing there," said Bill.

"Later. John Hale is in the living room."

"We've been looking for him. Lead the way."

Agatha introduced them. John, who had got to his feet, sank back onto the sofa looking miserable.

Bill questioned him closely. John's moving rapidly up the list of suspects, thought Agatha. John explained that he was at home, marking exam papers, when Gwen Simple had phoned with the bad news. He knew Mrs. Raisin had been hired to investigate and he had given her tickets for the theatre and so he had called on her to find out more. Bill asked if there were any witnesses to the fact that he said he had been home all that evening. He gave the names of two parents who had phoned him during the time the show was onstage.

He's frightened, thought Agatha. Wait a bit. He said one of the parents who phoned him was Mr. Buxton. That must be Kimberley's father. Should she tell Bill? Or was she going to protect John?

She suddenly realised Bill's shrewd almond eyes were fastened on her face. "What is it, Agatha?" he asked.

Slowly and reluctantly, Agatha said, "Mr. Buxton is the father of Kimberley, a pupil at John's school. The girl initially claimed Bert Simple had molested her, but now says he didn't. Toni tried to get something out of the girl but had no luck."

"Buxton called on me at the school," said John.

"So what did Mr. Buxton want?"

"He was angry with me," said John. "He blamed me for telling Agatha about Kimberley."

"Did he threaten you?"

"As a matter of fact, he did. He said if I didn't keep my mouth shut, I'd end up like

Bert Simple."

"You should have phoned the police immediately," said Bill severely.

"If I phoned the police every time a parent threatened me, I'd never be off the phone," said John wearily. "If their little genius — in their opinion — turns out to be failing English exams, they take it out on me."

"I would like you to call at police headquarters in the morning," said Bill, "and sign a statement."

"Of course."

After Bill had left, John rose and stretched. "What a horrible mess," he said. "I hope they lock up George and throw away the key."

Agatha escorted him to the door and helped him into his coat. He bent down and kissed her on the cheek. "Thank you for not calling me a fool," he said. "I owe you a meal. I'm a good cook. What about next Saturday evening?"

Looking up into his handsome face, Agatha forgot about any doubts about him. "I'd love to. What time?"

"Eight o'clock. Here's my card with my address." He kissed her on the cheek again. Agatha opened the door. Tiny snowflakes were beginning to swirl in the light over the door.

"I'd better get home before this gets worse," said John. "See you soon."

Agatha dreamily watched him go.

The newspapers and television were full of the fake-head story on the following day. Agatha finally locked her office door to keep the press out. Interest in the gruesome murder of Bert Simple had been reanimated and she knew Winter Parva would be full of the media.

She settled down at her desk to read the newspaper reports. Gwen Simple was reported as being too distressed to make a statement. Other members of the cast were threatening to sue George for causing them post-traumatic stress.

Agatha turned to Patrick. "See if any of your police contacts can let you know if George has been charged."

Patrick put on his coat and left the office. Agatha looked out of the window. The snow was coming down thicker. If she did not make a move soon, she would not get to Winter Parva.

But if she did go to try to see if George had been released and returned home, the press would all be waiting outside the gift shop.

Mrs. Freedman was patiently answering the phone and reading from a typed statement.

"Agatha Raisin was at the performance and witnessed the whole thing. George Southern begged to replace John Hale for one performance only. Mrs. Raisin does not know why he decided on such a horrible trick. Goodbye."

The calls grew less and finally ceased.

Toni appeared and said it looked as if most of the roads were going to be impassable. She was soon followed by Simon and Phil, complaining about the same thing.

They all sat, drinking coffee, and watching the white world outside the windows. Patrick appeared at last, shaking snow from his heavy overcoat. "George has been kept in overnight," he said, "and they're going to be interviewing him again today. Evidently Wilkes thinks that someone who could go to the lengths of performing such a macabre joke probably killed Bert."

"I believe members of the cast are threatening to sue him for causing post-traumatic stress," said Agatha.

"The actual charge," said Patrick, "would be nervous shock and they would need to pay a psychiatrist to back up the claim. Is there anything else I can do?"

"I don't think there's anything any one of us can do until they get the gritters out," said Agatha. "You can all go."

"I don't think I'll make it to Carsely," said Phil.

There was a knock at the office door and a familiar voice called, "Agatha!"

Agatha rushed to open the door. James Lacey, her former husband, stood there, smiling at her.

"How did you get here?" asked Agatha. "Let me take your coat."

"I've invested in a Land Rover with snow tyres," said James. "I've been reading all about the Winter Parva case and wondered if you needed any help."

"Oh, that would be great," said Agatha. She studied James. He was as handsome as ever. Then she remembered how difficult their marriage had been. And James had been furious when Agatha had insisted on keeping the name Raisin, that of her first husband, for business. Then her racing mind thought, I must get rid of him by next Saturday. I don't want anyone messing up my date with John.

Aloud, she said, "We could drop Phil back off in Carsely and go on to Winter Parva from there. Toni, Simon, you've both got digs close by so you can go now."

Young Toni blushed slightly as she passed James, remembering when she had once had a crush on him.

Simon hurried after her. James sat down next to Agatha at her desk.

"I've been looking at my notes," said Agatha, "and I've just remembered something. Gareth Craven, the producer of the pantomime who's hired me to investigate, well, he told me he wanted to marry Gwen Simple but that he was married at the time.

"But Bessie Burdock was the one who told us that Gareth had rushed off to get married *after* Gwen got married. It's a small lie, but it's a lie all the same."

"Maybe he was just trying to save face," said James. "But I'd like to meet this Gareth Craven."

"We'll go in a minute," said Agatha. "I've got Toni's notes here. I hadn't time to read them. She thinks Kimberley really wanted to tell her something but her father was making threatening noises and she clammed up. She plans to go back and try to get Kimberley on her own."

"So let's brave the snow," said James, "and see what Gareth has to say for himself."

The main roads had been gritted but it was

hard going on the untreated country roads leading to Winter Parva. Agatha covertly studied James and wondered what he was thinking. His handsome face seemed inscrutable. Did he ever think of the nights in bed they had spent when they were married? Probably not, thought Agatha, feeling suddenly frumpy and deflated.

"Isn't this that village where they roasted a cop at the pig roast?" asked James.

"The very one," said Agatha. As they drove along the main street, she said, "Just look at it. Like a picture postcard. I can't help wondering what goes on behind those net curtains and closed doors. Probably husbands beating the shit out of their wives."

"Cynic," commented James.

"Slow down," said Agatha. "It's that house over there."

There was no reply when they rang the doorbell.

"Could it be that he is in Mircester getting ready to put the show on again?" asked James.

"He might," said Agatha. "He has to get back the money that was paid back on the first night. But before we go back, I'd like to see if George Southern has been released

90

by the police. The gift shop is in the main street. It's right next to the post office."

They drove to the gift shop. There was a Closed notice on the door.

"Probably still being grilled by the police," said James.

"Surely not." Agatha peered out of the car. The snow had turned to large flakes, drifting slowly down. "Wait a moment. There's a light on upstairs."

They got out and went up to the shop door. James hammered on it and the door slowly opened. A chorus of "Behold the Lord High Executioner" sounded from above.

"Let's go up," said Agatha.

"It's trespass," said the ever-cautious James.

"We'll shout."

Agatha began yelling, "Mr. Southern!"

"He'll never hear you," said James. "He's playing the music awfully loudly."

Agatha lifted the counter and made her way through to the back shop. "Look! There are stairs leading up," she said.

"I really don't think . . ." began James, but Agatha was already mounting the stairs.

She pushed open the door at the top, releasing a blast of sound.

Agatha was about to walk in when she

stopped short and let out a whimpering sound. She turned round and collided with James.

"It's awful," she said.

He put his arms round her. "What's awful?"

"His head is on his living room floor and there's blood everywhere."

"Let me see. The idiot's probably playing another stupid trick."

He released Agatha and edged past her.

James saw the head, the blood and the bloody executioner's sword lying on the carpet.

"Let's get out of here. Call the police."

He helped her down the stairs and into the Land Rover after he had called the police.

"Oh, James," wailed Agatha. "I have seen some terrible sights in my career but I think this is the worst."

He put an arm round her. "The police will soon be here. We'll make our statements and go back to Carsely where you can have a warm drink."

At one point it seemed as if the police would never arrive but then Wilkes, Bill Wong and Alice Peterson drove up in a police Land Rover. "I'll deal with this," said James, getting out of his vehicle.

But Agatha got out as well, telling herself she was a detective and to get a grip.

The snow had suddenly stopped and a pale sun shone down through a break in the clouds.

James rapidly told Wilkes what they had seen.

"Detective Sergeant Peterson will take your statements," said Wilkes. James saw a pub opposite.

"We'll go over to the pub," he said.

"Very well," said Wilkes. "But stay there until I join you."

"You should really have hot sweet tea," admonished James as Agatha clutched a large gin and tonic.

"Hate the stuff," said Agatha, taking a gulp of her drink.

James described what they had seen while Alice recorded his statement on tape and also wrote it down in her notebook.

When it was Agatha's turn, she felt it was like describing a nightmare.

"Do you think that was the sword from the theatre?" asked Alice.

"I don't know," said Agatha. "There's some awful hate-filled person around. To play that music!"

At last Wilkes and Bill joined them. "The forensic team are going over everything," said Wilkes.

"Did you find the rest of the body?" asked Agatha.

"It was in the corner of his living room behind the sofa. It looks as if someone sliced his head off while he was asleep. What is even more horrible, is that there was a CD of the executioner's chorus. Someone had programmed it to play over and over again. You will now need to go with Peterson to police headquarters and wait until your statements are prepared and then sign them."

On the road to Mircester, James suddenly swung into a lay-by and stopped the car.

"Agatha, I want you to drop this case," he said.

"I've never dropped a case yet," said Agatha. "Why?"

"Because this mad murderer might come after you."

"James," said Agatha wearily, "I will put it on hold. By tomorrow or even later today, the village of Winter Parva will be thick with the media and tomorrow, the world's media will join them. There will be squads of police going from door to door. I won't be able to get near anyone."

"I really do wish you would drop it."

"No and no. Drive on."

After they were finished signing their statements, James left Agatha at her office. She waited until her small staff had all come back, complaining about the difficulty of getting anywhere through the snow.

Agatha told them about the latest gruesome murder. "I had better phone Gareth Craven," she said finally. "I won't be able to proceed with any investigation while the village is flooded with police, rubber-neckers and the whole of the world's media. You can all go home. We'll do what we can tomorrow. This snow can't last forever."

After they had all left, Agatha phoned Gareth Craven. He sounded frantic. "I can't take much more of this. Haven't you the slightest idea who is doing this?"

"Not yet. But I will, I promise you," said Agatha with a confidence she did not feel. "I will be back on the job once the press hysteria cools. I called on you before I found George but you weren't at home."

"I was out at an old neighbour's shovelling snow."

"I tried your mobile."

Gareth gave a shaky laugh. "I'd left it at

home. What is this? Am I a suspect?"

"No," said Agatha quickly. "I just wondered if you had seen anything or heard anything."

"I wish I had. I must try to see Gwen. This is awful for her."

"Let me know what she or anyone else says," said Agatha.

She had just put down the phone when it rang. It was John Hale. Agatha's heart gave a lurch.

"This is awful, horrible," said John. "I'm in Mircester. May I call on you?"

"Yes, of course," said Agatha. "But aren't you on stage tonight?"

"We were going to perform as usual but the police said the theatre must be closed down. Be with you in a few minutes. I'll tell you all about it."

After she had rung off, Agatha slid out the bottom drawer of her desk and took out a magnifying mirror and a bag of make-up. She cleaned off her old make-up and put on a fresh layer and then brushed her hair until it crackled with electricity. Her black cashmere sweater was all right, she decided, as were her black tapered trousers, but she was wearing flat-soled boots, and, without heels on, Agatha felt demoralised.

As she waited for John, Agatha began to

wonder uneasily about him. Why had he allowed George to take his place?

But when John walked in, Agatha surveyed all that masculine beauty and forgot about her doubts.

"Do sit down," she said. "Have the police been questioning you?"

"Over and over again," said John.

"Why at the theatre?"

"Evidently it was the executioner's sword that killed George."

"But these stage swords are surely made of wood," said Agatha.

"This one was steel. It had been made razor sharp."

"How does Blain explain the sharp sword?"

"He said it was as dull as anything during rehearsals," said John.

"I wonder if the blacksmith sharpened it," said Agatha.

"I'm sure the police will think of that. I owe you dinner."

Agatha's phone rang. "I'd better answer that in case it's the police again."

But it was Mrs. Bloxby. "Such awful weather," said the vicar's wife. "But the farmers have cleared the road down to the village and the A44 has been salted and gritted. I left a lamb casserole on your doorstep.

All you need to do is heat it up."

Agatha thanked her and turned to John. "That was my friend, Mrs. Bloxby. She's left one of her famous lamb casseroles for me. Why don't you come back with me and we'll have dinner at my place?"

"I'd love to, but I don't have snow tyres," said John.

"I do," said Agatha, her mind full of romance. "I'll run you to Carsely and then take you home."

Agatha's head was crowded with dreams as she drove home. She would suggest he stay the night . . . and then . . . and then . . .

The casserole was on the doorstep under a wooden box. Agatha carried it in, lit the oven and put it in.

James, who had been worried about her, had seen her arrival from his window. He phoned Charles.

"Agatha has just arrived home with an exceptionally handsome man. Do you know who he is?"

"Haven't a clue," said Charles. "I may run over and join the party. Maybe later."

Agatha and John had a pleasant dinner. Agatha had found a good bottle of wine and then produced a bottle of brandy. John seemed to enjoy chatting about the school and Agatha loved watching his face.

Then he said, "We've been drinking rather a lot. Do you think you can really drive me home?"

"Why not stay the night?" said Agatha. "I have a spare room."

He smiled. "I am rather tired."

"I can take you back in the morning."

Bustling about in a housewifely way, quite unlike her usual behaviour, Agatha found him clean towels and one of Charles's dressing gowns he had left behind on his last visit.

She stood hopefully outside his bedroom door. "I hope you have a good night's sleep," she said.

"I'm sure I will." He bent down, kissed her on the cheek and retreated into the spare room.

"Snakes and bastards," muttered Agatha, stumping off to her own bedroom.

She lay awake for a long time, nursing hopes that he might join her, but at last fell into a heavy sleep.

Charles Fraith let himself into Agatha's cottage shortly after midnight. He was tired. His aunt's dinner party seemed to have gone on forever. He yawned and opened the door to the spare bedroom and switched on the light. He stared at the man in the bed, switched off the light and retreated.

He opened Agatha's door. The moon shining in the window showed Agatha asleep on one side of her double bed. He shrugged, then stripped off his clothes and climbed in beside her. He folded his hands neatly on his chest and soon was sound asleep.

John awoke early. He phoned his headmaster to find the school was closed because of the snow. He tried to go back to sleep, but decided instead to get up and go downstairs for a cup of coffee.

He put a bath towel over his arm and headed for the bathroom. It was locked. He was just turning away when the bathroom door opened. He swung round. A naked man was surveying him.

"Good morning," said Charles. "We haven't been introduced. I am Charles Fraith. And you are?"

"John Hale."

"Ah, the schoolteacher. I'd better get dressed. I'm sleeping in Agatha's other spare room. Practically a cupboard. See you downstairs."

Charles walked past him but waited until John had gone into the bathroom. He went into Agatha's bedroom and hurriedly dressed. Agatha was still asleep. When he was dressed, he shook her awake.

"What the hell are you doing here?" demanded Agatha.

"Hush. I met your inamorato. I told him I had slept in the other spare room."

"You know there isn't one. Where did you sleep?"

"Beside you, my sweeting."

"Damn you! I am taking those keys I gave you back, once and for all. Get the hell out of here!"

"Not till I have had coffee. And I have news for you. The chief constable came for dinner last night."

Agatha heard John leaving his room. "Say you're one of my detectives," she hissed.

John made his way down to the kitchen. He had not told Agatha he had been married and had a son. He found the alimony and child maintenance he had to pay left him with not very much money. Agatha was obviously rich. Her cottage was well appointed. A rich wife could ease the burden.

Agatha dressed hurriedly and went downstairs, just in time to hear the doorbell ring. When she opened the door, James was standing on the step.

"Oh, come on in and join the party," said Agatha crossly. "Why don't you invite the whole village?"

And with that, she turned her back on him, leaving him to close the door and follow her into the kitchen.

John, she saw to her dismay, was freshly shaved. He must have used one of her razors. She turned red with embarrassment.

"I took the liberty of taking a clean shirt out of the wardrobe in the spare room. And I found an electric razor in one of the drawers."

"This is my ex-husband, James Lacey," said Agatha, not wanting Charles to say he left spare clothes in the spare room. She hadn't known about the razor because her cleaner, Doris Simpson, always cleaned that room along with the others.

"James, this is John Hale. He was supposed to be in *The Mikado* the night George Southern took his place."

"Doesn't anyone want to hear my great news?" asked Charles, taking one of Agatha's cigarettes and lighting it.

"Out with it," commanded Agatha.

"David Buxton has been taken in for questioning."

"How did you find that out?" asked Agatha.

"As I said, the chief constable was at a dinner party last night. He said Buxton took the sword to the blacksmith and had it ground until it was razor sharp. He then showed off to some of the chorus, showing it was so sharp it could slice a dropped scarf in half. He said he did it to surprise Colin Blain."

"And has he confessed?"

"Not a bit of it, says it was a joke. But wasn't his daughter supposed to have been sexually assaulted by Bert Simple?"

"That's right. If only it can turn out to be him," said Agatha. "On the other hand, I am being paid to investigate and if the police solve the murder, I won't get any money."

"I'm surprised at you, Agatha," said John. "Think of poor Gwen. It would be marvellous for her to have closure."

"I don't give a sod for poor Gwen," said Agatha. "She may have committed the murders herself."

"And with that, love flew out the window," murmured Charles.

"If you don't mind," said John stiffly, "I would like to get back to Mircester."

"Of course, I'll drive you," said Agatha. "Do let yourself out, Charles, and lock up behind you. I expect you to report to the office later and type up a report."

"Is Charles one of your detectives?" asked John.

"Yes," said Charles at the same time as James said, "No."

"Part time," said Charles airily. "Off you go."

CHAPTER FIVE

John was silent for part of the journey to Mircester. Who was this Charles Fraith? He had not expected any competition if he decided to pursue Agatha. But there was a strange rapport between her and this Charles. And he hadn't liked the suspicious looks her ex had been giving him. But Agatha was not only attractive but rich.

"I am afraid we didn't have a very good date. And now I owe you a meal. Why don't you come to my place for dinner tomorrow night instead of waiting until Saturday?"

"I'd love that," said Agatha.

"I gave you my card. I've got a flat in Mircester near the theatre."

"That would be lovely," said Agatha, happy again. "And look, it's beginning to thaw and the sun has come out."

John's mobile phone rang. Agatha heard him say, "I can be with you in about fifteen minutes." When he rang off, he said, "That was the police. They want to interrogate me again."

"Do you want me to come with you?"

"No, I'll be all right."

But Agatha could sense his uneasiness. The police would want to question him once more about why he gave up his starring role on opening night to George Southern.

"I often wonder," she said cautiously, "why you let George take your place."

"Because I am too soft-hearted," said John. "He begged and begged until I gave in."

John did not want her to know the truth, the truth being that George had paid him a thousand pounds to take his place. He certainly did not want Agatha to know how desperate he was for money.

Agatha bought all the morning newspapers before she went to the office. She told her staff to get on with whatever cases they were working on, with the exception of Toni who she asked to stay behind. Agatha often had to fight down feelings of jealousy for her beautiful assistant until common sense told her that Toni was the brightest and best.

"Take half these papers, Toni," said Agatha, "and go through them and compare them with my notes on the computer and see if there is anything I might have missed. Now, there is a schoolteacher called John Hale. I don't want you to go near him, but I want you to find out some background on him. After all, why would he give up his place in *The Mikado* to George Southern?"

Toni took away half the newspapers, and Agatha settled back with a sigh. Her ongoing low self-worth made her cautious. She could not quite accept that John was interested in her because he found her attractive. Other people might judge Agatha's appearance to be that of an attractive woman, but Agatha always wished she looked younger, thinner and glamorous.

The newspapers were full of the gruesome story of the beheading of George. There was a long interview in the *Daily Mail* with Gareth Craven. "Shock upon shock and blah, blah, blah," muttered Agatha. She read on. Gwen Simple and her son had declared themselves too upset to speak to the press. Pixie Turner was only given one line and no photo. She'll be furious, thought Agatha.

Toni suddenly said, "You were asking about John Hale?"

"Yes. What?" asked Agatha.

"There's a bit about him in *The Guardian*. It says he is not available for comment. The reporter says there is a mystery as to why he let George Southern take his place in *The Mikado.* He was not to be found at home or at the home of his ex-wife, Olivia."

"Let me see that," said Agatha sharply. Toni handed the newspaper to Agatha, open at the article. Agatha quickly read it. John's ex-wife lived in Oxford. Agatha raised her eyebrows. He had a son. Olivia was quoted as having said that she had not seen her husband for four years. Any communication was done through her lawyer.

Why had he not told her about his ex-wife and son? But then, she had not told him about her first marriage, which had dramatically ended in murder. She conjured up a picture of John's beauty. Oh, what prestige to have a husband who looked like that!

"Thanks," she said gruffly and turned to the other newspapers. "Here's something interesting in *The Times,* Toni. That blacksmith was the one who sharpened the sword. I'd like another word with him when all the fuss dies down. I won't be able to get near anyone at the moment until the press go away again."

"Do you want me to try to see John Hale?" asked Toni.

"No!" said Agatha sharply. "But what we could do is try to see Gareth Craven. I'd like to know what you make of him. If there are too many press around his door, we'll leave it."

The temporary thaw was over and piles of dingy slush were piled up on either side of the roads. The sky was dark grey and more snow was forecast. Agatha drove both of them to Winter Parva. She was wearing a body stocking for the first time. She had enjoyed looking at her slim figure in the mirror that morning but now her skin under the body stocking was beginning to itch and she felt uncomfortable and constricted.

Satellite dishes, cables and television vans littered the main street of Winter Parva. There were very few journalists in sight. "They're probably in the pub somewhere," said Agatha.

"This early?" said Toni.

"It's bang on eleven o'clock," remarked Agatha. "The witching hour for all of the media. Here we are at Gareth's place and not a reporter in sight. Let's see what he has to say for himself."

They rang the bell. "Go away!" shouted a voice from inside.

Agatha bent down and called through the letterbox. "It's me. Agatha."

There came the sound of the door being unlocked. Gareth opened it and said urgently, "Come in. I thought you were the press."

Agatha introduced Toni. "You are much too beautiful to be a detective," beamed Gareth.

"Why, thank you," said Agatha sarcastically. "The latest I've heard from the newspapers is that George Southern had that sword sharpened by the blacksmith."

"That's right. The silly man was fooling around with it."

"But what did the man who played the part of the Lord High Executioner have to say about it?"

"Colin Blain. It seems he was in on the joke. They meant people to get a fright afterwards. He said he never thought the girls would look at it on the stage. We're going to open again next week and I'm glad to say that we're fully booked until the end of the run. We'll be able to make up our losses."

"But won't some members of the cast be too frightened?" asked Toni.

"No. They're all elated at the thought of big audiences and press coverage," said Gareth.

"May I use your bathroom?" asked Agatha.

"Up the stairs on the left."

Agatha hurried up to the bathroom, went in and locked the door. She stripped off, removed the body stocking and stuffed it into her capacious handbag and had a luxurious scratch before putting her clothes on again.

She arrived back downstairs in time to hear Toni saying, "I cannot understand what made your leading man give up his place to George Southern."

"Neither can I," said Gareth. "Particularly as everyone believes John is sweet on Gwen."

"Well, he'll be able to marry her now," commented Toni, suddenly aware of a gimlet stare from Agatha and wondering what she had done wrong.

But she went on, "Was George Southern in the way of playing practical jokes?"

"I'm afraid so. Some of them could be quite cruel."

"Such as?" asked Agatha.

"Oh, stupid things. In the ladies' toilet at the town hall, he put cling film over the lavatory pans. He put pepper into the powder bowl so Pixie Turner had a violent fit of sneezing and all her make-up had to be done again. Things like that. Pixie threatened to kill him. But then we all did at one time or another."

"My money's on the blacksmith," said Agatha. "Anyone been charged with anything?"

"Colin Blain has been charged with carrying a dangerous weapon. But at the moment, it's John who is the prime suspect."

"Why?" asked Agatha.

"Well, George would never have got the part otherwise and played that trick which obviously annoyed someone so much that they murdered him."

"But I don't see how that makes John Hale guilty. He's been married and is no doubt paying alimony on a teacher's salary," said Toni. "Maybe George Southern paid him something."

Agatha began to wish she had not brought Toni. She did not want her romantic dreams of being married to a gorgeous man dimmed by suspicion.

Gareth interrupted her thoughts by asking, "As a detective, you do have a license?"

"Never needed one," said Agatha.

"You will soon," said Gareth. "You will need to be licensed by the Security Agency Authority and go on a training course."

"But I don't need a training course," exclaimed Agatha. "I have a great track record."

"It's soon to be the law," said Toni.

"And how on earth is the work of the

agency supposed to be done while we're all on training courses," complained Agatha.

"I'm sure we'll cope somehow," said Toni. "I read about it. It's because they claim there are a lot of rogue agencies tapping into phones and paying for access to bank accounts. The press don't know why they should have been singled out for criminal prosecution when some detective agencies were guilty of phone hacking as well."

Agatha turned her mind back to the case. "Gareth," she urged, "think hard. It's maybe someone in the theatre. If anyone is mad and vicious enough to plan and execute these murders, you must have some idea."

"I haven't," said Gareth. "Amateur companies are often full of inflated egos and quarrels do start, but I cannot think of someone so full of hate."

They could get nothing interesting out of him and eventually took their leave.

Outside, Winter Parva was living up to its name. It was a bitterly cold day. An icy wind had sprung up.

"What now?" asked Toni.

"I'm afraid all we can do at the moment," said Agatha, "is go back to the office and work on all our other cases until the interest in this one dies down. Then we'll come back and check out everyone again."

■ ■ ■ ■

Agatha was relieved that evening to find that
Charles had decided not to stay. She got a
phone call from her former employee, Roy
Silver, saying he hoped to be down at the
week-end, but Agatha put him off. What if
her date with John could lead to something?
She told Roy to wait until the following
week-end.

The following day, she found it hard to
concentrate on her work.

More snow was forecast so she had
brought a small suitcase with a change of
clothes into the office. She dreamt that it
would snow hard and John would be obliged
to put her up for the night.

By five o'clock it had started to snow hard.
She told her staff to go home. But Toni and
Simon remained. Toni said she had notes to
type up and Simon was waiting hopefully
for her to finish so he could invite her for a
drink.

By six o'clock, Agatha said impatiently,
"Do go home. I'm going to lock up."

"Be leaving shortly," said Toni.

"Just go now!" ordered Agatha.

What an infuriating length of time it
seemed to take Toni to close down her

114

computer and put on her coat. At last she and Simon went off and Agatha was free to change her clothes and put on fresh make-up. She looked out at the falling snow and decided gloomily that she would need to wear serviceable boots. But she put a pair of red suede shoes with low heels in her bag. She decided her silk scarlet blouse with the low neckline worn over a black flared skirt was pretty enough, but it would need to be buried under a thick cardigan.

When she finally left the office, she found to her dismay that it was snowing hard and that her car seemed almost buried. Agatha took out a brush and cleared the snow. Fortunately, hers was about the only car on the road as she battled her way to John's apartment, which was in an old building near the theatre.

She pressed the bell marked HALE, and when the buzzer sounded walked in and up the stairs with a feeling of excitement that mounted every step she took.

John's flat was on the second floor and he was waiting by the open door when she arrived.

"Welcome," he said. "Let me take your coat and hat."

Agatha pulled off her fur hat, hoping her hair hadn't been too flattened by it. Then her coat, cardigan and boots. She took out the red shoes and slipped them on.

It was only when John ushered her into the living room that she realised the place was cold. The living room was small. A dining table had been set by the window. Bookshelves lined the walls. It was like a library. In the centre of the room was a small sofa and one armchair.

Agatha shivered. "Don't you have any heating?" she asked.

John was wearing a thick blue sweater the colour of his eyes. "I find it pretty warm," he said. "Let me get you your cardigan."

"I'd rather have some heat," said Agatha stubbornly, not wanting to eclipse the glory of her silk blouse.

He went to a thermostat in the wall and turned it up. A dusty old radiator against a space in one wall which was not covered in books let out a series of cracks as it heated up.

"I meant to bring you some wine," said Agatha, "but with this awful weather, I forgot."

"It doesn't matter," said John, although he had been hoping she would bring some wine. "Gin?"

"Yes, please," said Agatha. He disappeared into the kitchen and returned shortly with a glass of gin and tonic. "I'm afraid I haven't any ice."

The gin and tonic was warm. Agatha thought he must keep the drinks next to the cooker.

"I'll just go and fix dinner," said John, going back into the kitchen. Agatha had a swig of gin and looked around. Apart from the kitchen door, there were two other doors leading off the living room. Agatha got to her feet and quietly opened one door. It was a small office with a desk, a computer and a typing chair. Agatha remembered Toni's speculation that George Southern might have paid John to take his place. She suddenly wondered if he kept his bank statements in his desk.

She heard the ping of a microwave coming from the kitchen and hurriedly closed the door and retreated to the living room.

"Dinner's ready!" called John. "Take a seat at the table."

Agatha did as she was told. She shook out a paper napkin. There was a bottle of red wine on the table without a label.

John came in, bearing two plates of lasagne. He slid a plate in front of Agatha and then sat down opposite her. "You must try this wine," he said. "A friend brought it back from Bulgaria." He poured her a glass.

Agatha finished her gin and cautiously took a sip of the wine. It was awful, sour and harsh.

After a forkful of the lasagne, Agatha, whom Charles had dubbed Queen of the Microwave, recognised it as being the cheapest variety anyone could buy.

They discussed the case, Agatha not learning anything new.

When the lasagne was finished, he smiled into Agatha's eyes. "Do you ever feel like settling down?" he asked.

"And stop detecting?"

"Oh, no. We've all got to work. I meant, do you ever feel you would like to get married?"

"Often," said Agatha. "But only if I meet the right person."

He took her hand in a warm clasp. "I am sure you will."

Damn Toni, thought Agatha. He's either mean or strapped for cash.

"Is there any coffee?" she asked.

"Of course." He released her hand.

When he went into the kitchen, Agatha darted into his office. There were some unopened letters on his desk. On top was one from the Midlands & Cotswold Bank. She hurriedly stuffed it down inside her knickers.

When John reappeared with a tray bearing two cups of coffee, a bottle of milk and a bag of sugar, Agatha was back at her seat at the table.

He might have made more of an effort, she thought. From now on, I'm going to serve milk in a jug and sugar in a bowl.

"I take mine black," she said. "Oh, may I use your bathroom?"

"Of course." He pointed to the door next to the office door. "Go through there. It's off the bedroom."

Agatha, once she was in the bathroom, fished the bank letter out of her knickers and sat down on the lid of the pan. The envelope flap had not been stuck down properly. She eased the flap open. It was a bank statement. Her heart plummeted. A week before George had taken on John's role in *The Mikado,* there was a deposit of one thousand pounds. Before that, he had only had two hundred pounds in his account.

She carefully sealed it up again. Somehow, she had to manage to replace it.

It dawned on her that John was probably wooing her for her money. And to think she had planned to spend the night.

She flushed the toilet and ran the taps before leaving the bathroom and returning to the living room.

John said, "As beautiful as ever, Agatha."

"Do you think I might have another cup of coffee?" asked Agatha. "I've let this one get cold."

"Sure. Won't be long."

Agatha waited until he had gone, tiptoed into the office, fished out the bank statement, smoothed the envelope and put it on his desk. She got back to her seat just in time.

"There you are," said John. "I took a look out of the kitchen window. It's blowing quite a blizzard. I'm afraid you are going to have to stay the night."

If only it weren't true, thought Agatha, but I think he wants a rich wife.

"I am sorry," she said. "That Bulgarian wine must have upset my stomach. I have to go to the bathroom again."

Once in the bathroom, she took out her phone and called Charles on his mobile. When he answered, she whispered urgently, "I'm at John Hale's. Flat five, Twelve Mircester Road. You've got to get me out of here!"

"Okay," said Charles. "You're lucky I'm in Mircester."

Charles was having dinner with friends.

"I'm sorry," he announced. "My aunt's ill. Got to go."

"You'll never get home in this weather," said his hostess.

"I can but try," said Charles. "Duty calls."

Agatha and John had moved to the sofa. He was sitting so close to her that his thigh was pressed against hers. Agatha's hormones were doing a war dance while her low self-esteem was telling them to lie down.

"I feel we have a lot in common," said John. "When shall we go to bed . . . darling?"

"I don't do casual sex," said Agatha.

"But this is not casual. My dearest, when I saw you walk into my classroom, I thought, this is the woman for me."

Agatha could feel herself weakening. Why not? It had been a long time. What was up with wanting a night with this beautiful man whatever his motives?

"Sorry, I've got to go to the loo again," said Agatha.

She frantically phoned Charles but his mobile was switched off.

When she returned, John's doorbell rang. "Ignore that," he said.

Agatha hesitated. She knew it was Charles. If he couldn't get in, he might call the police, thinking something awful had happened to her.

"I think you should answer it," she said firmly. "It might be the police."

He got to his feet reluctantly, and pressed the bell to release the downstairs door.

Agatha could hear John saying sarcastically, "What an unexpected pleasure. What brings you here?"

And Charles's voice coming closer. "I've come to rescue Agatha. I've got the four-by-four. She'll never make it home in her own car."

Charles strolled into the room. "Hi, Aggie. I've come to give you a lift home."

"How did you know she was here?" demanded John.

"I told him," said Agatha quickly. "May I have my coat, please?"

John fetched her coat from the bedroom and her cardigan and boots. Both men stood silently while Agatha got dressed.

"Well, thank you for a delightful evening," said Agatha. "We must do this again."

"When?" asked John.

"I'll phone you. Bye. Come along, Charles."

"So," said Charles, as he drove cautiously through the snow, "why are you fleeing from Adonis back there?"

Agatha sighed. "He is beautiful, isn't he? That wretched Toni."

"What's Toni got to do with it? Did she lure him away?"

"No, she said that maybe George Southern had paid John to take his place on opening night. It stuck in my head. I took a peek in his bank statement. A week before the performance, John received a deposit of one thousand pounds. Before that, he had only two hundred in his account. Toni said that maybe he was strapped for cash. He's been married before and has a son."

"You'd better tell Bill Wong. So do you think he was after your money?"

"I don't want to," said Agatha miserably. "But it was an awful dinner. Cheap microwave lasagne and Bulgarian wine that tasted like paint stripper. No starter or dessert. I don't want to tell Bill. It's my investigation."

"If you don't and if there's another murder, and the murderer does turn out to be John, you'll never forgive yourself."

"I'll phone him tomorrow," said Agatha.

"I rescued you early. It's only ten thirty. Phone him when we get back. You can't look at his bank statements, but the police can, and they can find out if that thousand pounds came from George Southern."

"It still doesn't make John a murderer,"

protested Agatha.

"It's still very odd. These amateur dramatic people take themselves very seriously. You know that, Agatha. He must need money very badly."

"I suppose so," mumbled Agatha.

Once back in her cottage, Agatha phoned Bill after getting through the usual battle of pleading with his formidable mother to let him come to the phone. He listened carefully and then said, "Good work, Agatha. We can do with any lead."

And Agatha, conscious of Charles listening to every word, said, "Actually, it was Toni who put me on to it. But I think you owe it to me. Let me know what you find out."

"I can't really do that, Agatha."

"Oh, yes you can. If it hadn't been for me you wouldn't even have thought of it."

When Agatha said goodnight and rang off, she stood for a moment looking sadly down at the phone. She remembered John's beauty and suddenly felt like a traitor.

Charles's voice made her jump. "Have you thought, Agatha, that a man like John with those incredible good looks might rouse strong passions in people? For example, obsessions in women and jealousy in men."

"Perhaps," said Agatha reluctantly.

"Or perhaps," Charles pursued, "beautiful John is the murderer. That bakery seems to be a thriving business and Gwen is an attractive woman. With her husband out of the way, she would be free to marry again."

"So why come after me?" demanded Agatha.

"Maybe he is scared. He needs money but he won't want to do anything that might make the police suspect him. You've got money. Marry you, bump you off after you've made your will and after a couple of years to allay suspicion and he'd be comfortably off."

Agatha sat down at the kitchen table. "Then why go to all this elaborate business? All John had to do was bump off his ex."

"True. But in that case he'd be first suspect. I'd like to talk to the ex. Why don't we both go over to Oxford tomorrow?"

"In this weather! We'll be lucky if we get out of the front door."

Charles went to the kitchen door and looked out through the glass. "It's stopped snowing. I've got snow tyres and the main roads will probably be gritted by the morning."

"Okay," agreed Agatha. She thought that, after all, it would be interesting to see what

125

sort of female John had been married to. "I took a note of her address."

They left the following morning and drove off into a silent, white countryside.

"We'd better take the road out through Burford," said Charles. "They're notoriously bad at gritting the Woodstock road."

Once through Burford and onto the dual carriageway, it was easier going. As they reached the outskirts of Oxford, the sun shone down, glittering on the blanket of snow that covered the gardens of the houses in Summertown.

Agatha thought about John and Charles thought about Agatha. It would be hopeless being married to her, he thought, not for the first time. He would never be able to trust her. Agatha would always be one woman looking for an obsession.

"It's down near the synagogue," said Agatha, studying a map.

"I think there's a good Lebanese restaurant close by," said Charles.

"In this weather," said Agatha, "I crave junk food."

"All right. Here's the address. Quite a handsome villa. I wonder if she owns all of it."

"You can't park here," said Agatha. "It's

resident parking only."

"They're not going to be around to ticket people in this weather," said Charles, driving neatly into the only free parking place on the street.

The steps up to the front door of the villa had not been cleared. Agatha was wearing ankle boots, but Charles had on a pair of green Wellingtons.

"You go first," said Agatha, "and I'll follow in your footsteps."

"Sounds like Good King Wenceslas," said Charles. "I wonder what this woman is like."

Did John dump her, or was it the other way round? wondered Agatha.

It was a tall Victorian villa with handsome stained-glass panels on the door. Charles rang the bell. Agatha stood behind him, suddenly nervous. John's ex was bound to be beautiful, a beauty that would make one middle-aged detective feel diminished.

The door opened and a small, dumpy woman stared at them. Her hair was in rollers and she was wearing a long droopy sweater over jeans. An incongruous pair of fluffy pink slippers decorated her feet.

The door began to close. "I'm not buying anything," she said sharply. "I don't believe in God and I have double glazing."

"Mrs. Hale," said Agatha quickly. "I am a

127

private detective, hired to investigate the murders in Winter Parva. Here is my card."

The door opened wide. "I don't see what it has to do with me," she said. "But I'm curious. Come in."

As they entered the shadowy hall, two young women came down the stairs. "Bye, Mrs. H.," said one. "Going to try to make it to college."

"In here," said Olivia Hale. She ushered them into a study lined with books. "I live on the ground-floor rooms and let the rest to students. If I waited for my ex to pay up on time, I'd starve."

She sat behind a large desk and indicated they should sit in two seats facing her. The room was cold. A fly-speckled mirror hung over a tiled fireplace. In one corner on a low table was a small television set with two cups and an electric coffee maker.

"So what brings you?" she asked. "Suspect John of murdering people?"

"We have to find out the background of everyone involved," said Agatha. "For example, have you any idea why John would step down from his part on opening night and let George Southern take his place?"

"Money, I should think," said Olivia. "He is a very greedy man."

Agatha's heart sank. She had been secretly

hoping to hear something good about John. Her rosy dream of marrying a gorgeous man finally disappeared.

"Was yours a bad marriage?" asked Charles.

"Not at first. It was fine until the money ran out. I had inherited a comfortable amount along with this house from my parents. I was so much in love, so dazzled that someone like me should snare such a beautiful man that I left the banking side to John, who insisted we have a joint account. He had told me he was well off and only continued schoolteaching because he felt committed to the job. So we had expensive foreign holidays and dined at the best restaurants. Then I had a baby. My son is seventeen now and will finish at Prince Edward's in June. It was when I insisted he went to a private school that the trouble started. John said a state school was good enough and the boy could come to his school. I did not tell him, but I called in at the bank to check our finances. There was practically nothing left.

"I confronted John with it, and he waffled and said I had enjoyed all the foreign holidays and so on as much as he. So I said, at least we had this house and could let rooms. He hit the roof and said we could sell it for at least a million. I felt betrayed. We had poisonous rows and that was when he said, 'You don't think I married you for your looks.' So I got a lawyer. An aunt died and left me some money. I didn't tell John. I opened a separate account. I realised it would be enough to pay for a conversion to this villa. He agreed to the divorce but I made sure to get him to agree to alimony and child support. But murder! Not John. He's too weak. I'm amazed he hasn't found another rich woman to take my place. But I was old-fashioned. Any other woman would probably have seen through him." Her eyes suddenly filled with tears. "I try to remember the good times but I can't. He has no interest in our son. He's a cold-hearted mercenary beast. And they call some women gold diggers!"

Agatha felt sad and wanted to get away from the villa. The study was filled with white light from the snow outside. She felt they were encased in a bubble of cold light, like figures in one of those glass snowstorms you found in gift shops.

"And you are really sure John could not be capable of murdering anyone?" asked Charles gently.

"No, but someday someone might murder him. God knows, I've dreamt about it often enough."

"You have my card," said Agatha. "If you think of anything, phone me."

As they drove off, Agatha said, "I need junk food."

"Don't you care about your waistline?" asked Charles.

"Not today."

"Do you think dear John might be our murderer?"

"No, it doesn't seem like it," said Agatha.

"But what if George Southern threatened to tell everyone about John taking money from him?"

"Not really enough motive."

"Well, try this on for size. What if Bert Simple was blackmailing him over something?"

"Too far-fetched," said Agatha. "Besides, he didn't have anything to do with the pantomime."

"No, but he didn't need to. Anyone like John could have got below that stage between the dress rehearsal and the actual performance."

"Oh, forget about John," snapped Agatha. "What about you and Gwen?"

"She tried to get me to call again, but I told her I was too busy."

131

"Aha!"

"Aha, what?"

"If she's chasing after you, then she's hardly the grieving widow."

"Oh, shut up about it all," said Charles. "One greasy spoon coming up. You'll get a breakthrough soon."

But as Agatha ploughed through a plate of egg, sausage, bacon and chips, she did not realise how long it would be before that breakthrough happened.

CHAPTER SIX

It was only on television detective shows, thought Agatha bleakly, as she stared out at yet another grey cold day in late spring, that cases were quickly solved.

Winter had moved into a dismal cold spring, and Patrick Mulligan told Agatha that, according to his police sources, there was still not even a hint of the identity of the murderer.

Agatha had reinterviewed as many people as she could think of, with the exception of John Hale.

The weird thing was, that as time went by, the residents of Winter Parva seemed to settle down to their usual ways and forget about the murders. It had happened to Agatha before on a previous case where a whole village had decided the murderer must have been some visiting lunatic. Perhaps, thought Agatha, it was because the idea that the murderer might be one of them was too awful to contemplate. She had reluctantly told Gareth Craven at the end of January that she could not go on charging him until she produced results.

She worked hard on various other cases. Charles had disappeared again and James Lacey was off on his travels.

She had one last try at interviewing the Buxton family to try to find out if Kimberley had really been sexually attacked but the girl's parents threatened to take her to court and charge her with harassment.

The weather continued as gloomy as Agatha's mood. She had put Roy Silver off several times, but finally decided to invite him because she was feeling lonely. Agatha always felt lonely when she was not in love with anyone.

Roy, a rather effeminate young man who had once worked for Agatha, arrived on the Saturday morning. To Agatha's relief, he was, for once, conservatively dressed. Roy, who worked for a public relations firm, was handling a new account for expensive men's shoes. Like a chameleon, Roy dressed according to whatever client he happened to be representing. If he were representing, say, a pop group, then he would have gelled, spiky hair and jeans torn at the knee.

"The weather is simply awful," said Agatha. "It's so cold that everything is late. I haven't even seen a daffodil, and what's that white blossom that's usually out by now?"

"Blackthorn," said Roy.

"How do you know that?" asked Agatha.

"I did PR for the *Country People* magazine. I learned ever such a lot of boring rural stuff. So how's murder?"

"Nothing," said Agatha. "I've tried and tried. Now, what can I do to entertain you?"

"There's a performance of *The Mikado* in Mircester this evening. We could go," said Roy. "You can point out all the suspects to me."

It was a full house. Agatha was lucky enough to get two last-minute cancellations.

Roy wondered if something would happen. He was addicted to publicity for himself and in the past had muscled in on Agatha's cases, just to get his photograph in the newspapers.

Edging forward on his seat, Roy whispered, "Who is that gorgeous man?"

"John Hale," said Agatha. "I'll tell you about him afterwards."

John and Gwen turned out to have beautiful voices. The performance went without a hitch, much to Roy's disappointment. He began to wish he had not come. The weather was dreary and Agatha's microwave cookery was awful.

To his relief, Agatha suggested they have dinner at a nearby Chinese restaurant. "Now, fill me in," said Roy.

"John Hale is a schoolteacher and a mercenary bastard," said Agatha. "He chased after me because he thought I was rich. The late George Southern paid him one thousand pounds to take his place on opening night. The police found that out. But John swore blind that George was repaying a loan. That it had nothing to do with letting George take the starring role. So back to square one. When George was murdered, John was in rehearsals and there was no way he could have done it.

"Now, Gwen Simple, wife of the first murdered man, showed no sign of grief or shock. But I can't see her as a murderer."

"She and John are sweet on each other," said Roy.

Agatha pointed a chopstick at him. "How can you know that?"

"Body chemistry. Bet you anything they've been to bed together."

Agatha was amazed to feel a pang of pure jealousy. She didn't want John, did she?

"Do you know where he lives?" asked Roy.

"Yes, he's got a flat near the theatre."

"Let's go and spy on him," said Roy eagerly. "They've got to take off their make-up. Hurry up and finish eating."

Agatha was just driving past the theatre when John came out with Gwen. She stopped and watched. John and Gwen walked to a parked car. John held the door open for Gwen and then got into the driving seat. When he moved off, Agatha followed.

"They're heading for Winter Parva," she said.

"So maybe he'll stay the night," said Roy.

"So what?" grumbled Agatha. "That won't get us any further."

"But it might give John a reason to murder her husband," said Roy.

At last, John stopped outside the bakery. He walked round and opened the passenger door and helped Gwen out. He walked up to the door of the bakery with her, said something, kissed her on the cheek and went back to his car.

"Now, that's what I call a waste of time," said Agatha.

Roy decided to leave first thing in the morning. Nothing was going to happen that might result in him getting his picture in the newspapers. He had driven himself to

Carsely instead of coming by train as he usually did.

When Agatha went downstairs in the morning, it was to find a note from Roy saying he had been called back to London. "I often wonder if that young man really likes me," said Agatha to her cats. "Or does he only come in the hope of getting some publicity for himself?"

She let her cats out into the garden and stood looking at another grey, cold day. A high wind was driving ragged clouds across the sky. Agatha felt lonely. She tried to contact Charles but was told by Gustav, his gentleman's gentleman, that he had gone abroad. It was Sunday, so the vicar's wife would be busy. She had a longing to go back to bed, pull the duvet over her head and wake up when dreary Sunday was over. She decided to sit down at her computer and go over all the notes and interviews on the Winter Parva murders.

The suspects were stacked up before her eyes, a sort of log jam of suspects without a single clue to break them up and throw up one suspicious person. Still, she tried making a list of likely murderers. She put Harry Crosswith top of the list. According to Patrick Mulligan's police sources, his wife was his only alibi for the time of George

Southern's death. Then there was David Buxton, Kimberley's father. Before she went on, she began to wonder if there was someone she hadn't even thought of. What about Colin Blain, who had played the role of the Lord High Executioner?

She checked in the phone book. There was a C. Blain listed in Winter Parva. With a feeling of being back in the hunt again, Agatha put on a warm coat and headed out.

Colin Blain lived on the housing estate on the edge of the village. His was a detached house of the kind that has two rooms upstairs and two down. Agatha rang the bell. She recognised Colin without his stage make-up because he had been the smallest member of the cast, being barely five feet tall. He had thinning hair, combed in strips across a freckled scalp. His blue eyes were watery and his face was dominated by a large bulbous nose.

"Yes?"

Agatha handed him her card and explained that she was still investigating the murders.

"I don't have anything to tell you that I haven't told the police," he said.

"Just a few questions," said Agatha. "Can we go inside? It's freezing out here."

"Oh, all right." He stood aside to let her

past and then opened a door in the small hallway and ushered her into a living room where a tall, mannish woman was watching television. "My wife," he said. "Darling, leave us alone for a minute. This is a detective."

"Not again," grumbled his wife, but she left them alone after switching off the television.

"I really want to know if it was your idea to get that sword sharpened," said Agatha.

"Sit down," he said.

Agatha sat on a battered sofa and Colin on an equally battered armchair. Threads were hanging off the side of the armchair as if a cat had been sharpening its claws on it.

"It was meant to be a bit of fun," said Colin. "I mean, make it a real executioner's sword for a laugh. I took some melons in and cut them up for the chorus before the show, demonstrating how sharp the sword was."

"And where did you put it afterwards?"

"I shut it in a cupboard in my dressing room. With all that fuss over the fake head, anyone could have gone in there."

"And you were in on the joke? I mean placing the box with the fake head on the stage?"

"Yes. The idea was they would look at it

140

when the curtain came down."

"The head was very lifelike," said Agatha. Did George make it?"

"Yes. He was awfully clever with papier-mâché. When we had a fair in the village last year, he constructed carnival heads. Some of the heads were of the villagers and very lifelike they were, too. Mind you, he annoyed a lot of people with his practical jokes."

"But can you think of anyone who would be annoyed enough to kill him?"

Colin shook his head.

"But what about the sword? Surely the police would take it away after the practical joke. They would regard it as a dangerous weapon."

"I think they forgot it. They were so fed up with us all and yakked on about wasting police time. So, like I said, I shut it up in the cupboard in my dressing room."

"George Southern was a bachelor?"

"No, he was married but the marriage broke up years ago."

"Does his wife live in Winter Parva?" asked Agatha.

"She lives in Mircester, or did do, the last I heard."

"Do you have an address for her?"

"No, but I 'member someone saying it was

in one of those tower blocks out by the industrial estate."

"What was her name before she got married?" asked Agatha.

"Alice Freemont."

Back in her car, Agatha checked on her iPad for the correct address. She found an A. Freemont listed at Haden Court, wrote down the address and headed back towards Mircester.

A group of tower blocks loomed up against the steel grey sky. Bits of rubbish blew across a parking lot outside Haden Court. To Agatha's relief, the lift worked, because she had discovered from studying a board at the entrance that Alice's flat was on the top floor. As she came out of the lift, the icy wind seemed to cut through to her very bones.

She hurried along the open corridor and rang the bell of Alice's flat, suddenly wishing she had phoned first.

The door was opened by a small woman whose features showed a sort of faded prettiness. Her brown hair was curly and her eyes, brown. She was wearing two sweaters over a pair of jeans.

Agatha introduced herself. "You'd better come in," said Alice. She had a soft, Gloucestershire accent.

The living room looked as if it had been furnished by Ikea. There were no books, pictures or photographs and everything was scrupulously clean.

"If you're here to ask about George, I can't help you," said Alice. "I can't think of anyone who might want to have murdered him."

"Why did your marriage break up?" asked Agatha.

"Do sit down."

Agatha sat on a sofa and Alice sat next to her.

"Fact is," said Alice, "it was because he wouldn't stop playing practical jokes. Even on our honeymoon, he put a rubber spider in the bed and gave me a fright. The odd thing is, I saw him a week before he died. He didn't have to pay alimony or anything like that. It was an amicable divorce. But he turned up saying he wanted us to get back together again. He said he was lonely. I told him I'd made a life for myself and I didn't want to marry him again. He said he was coming into money . . . ."

"How?" asked Agatha.

"He didn't say. But he said he was going to sell the gift shop and we could go abroad."

"Did you think the money he was talking

about was to come from the gift shop?"

"I can't understand it. I know he took out a second mortgage."

Agatha scowled horribly in thought. At last she said slowly, "Just suppose George knew the identity of the murderer and was blackmailing him. Is that possible?"

"He certainly was always short of money. But I can't believe he would do something so dangerous. He might just have confided in that girl who worked for him, Molly Kite."

"I'll try her. Do you know her address?"

"I think I still have it somewhere." Alice left the room and returned shortly with a bulky address book. She turned the pages and then said, "Here she is. Number five, The Loaming. It's a little road that runs along the back of the high street."

Feeling she might be getting somewhere at last, Agatha drove back to Winter Parva. At first, Agatha thought that Alice had made a mistake. The Loaming seemed to have nothing more than sheds, no doubt belonging to the shops on the high street. But right at the end, she found a small brick cottage.

Agatha knocked at the door. A dingy lace curtain on a window on the right twitched and then she could hear shuffling footsteps.

The door was opened by a squat man in his pyjamas. He smelled strongly of beer. His sparse hair stood on end.

"Does Molly Kite live here?" asked Agatha.

"She's at work."

"Where's work?"

"You the social?"

"I'm a private detective," said Agatha, wishing for the hundredth time she had the power of the police.

"Works at Jacey's supermarket, her does," he said and slammed the door.

Agatha shouted through the letter box, "Which Jacey's?" Jacey's was a chain of supermarkets.

A faint voice reached her ear. "Mircester."

Agatha got back into her car and drove off, switching on the heater as she did so. As she drove up out of Winter Parva, she suddenly saw a small clump of snowdrops by the roadside and felt cheered. Surely the cold days must be coming to an end.

Jacey's was on the outskirts of Mircester. Agatha really meant to park her car as far away from the entrance as she could, as that way she could get some exercise, but the day was so cold, she slid into a space nearest the front doors.

Once more she wished she were a police

officer. If she were, she could ask for the manager and demand that Molly be brought to her. Instead she headed for the customer services desk and asked to speak to Molly. She had to state her business and was told that Miss Kite would be on her break in half an hour. If Mrs. Raisin would take a seat, they would see whether she was willing to talk to her.

So Agatha sat on a chair by the entrance, suffering in the blasts of cold air that flooded in every time the automatic doors opened. A figure suddenly loomed over her and a cultured voice said, "I know you from somewhere." Agatha looked up. A tall man stood there, holding a plastic bag of groceries. He had a square, pleasant face, thick grey hair and brown eyes. He was wearing a Barbour with a red scarf tucked in at the neck.

"I don't think so," said Agatha cautiously.

"I know. I'm a friend of James Lacey. You were married to him, weren't you? I was a guest at your wedding." His face crinkled up in an attractive smile. Agatha's spirits soared.

"I was thinking of going for a drink," he said. "Feel like joining me, or are you waiting for someone?"

"Just resting," said Agatha, consigning her

appointment with Molly to the devil.

"There's a pub just along the road," he said. "I'll drive us and then bring you back to your car."

Damn this awful weather, thought Agatha. I'm sure my nose is red and these flat-heeled boots make me feel dumpy. He led the way to a Land Rover.

"Still detecting?" he asked.

"Oh, yes. What about you?" asked Agatha.

"I'm a farmer. Got a place not far from here."

"I didn't think farmers would shop in supermarkets," said Agatha. "I mean, when it comes to supplying local produce, they're not very loyal."

"It's handy for a few things. Here we are." He drove into the car park of a pub called The Dog and Duck.

He got out and went round and helped Agatha get down. Is he being a gentleman, she fretted, or does he think I am old? How old is he? Despite the grey hair, I think he's about my age.

The pub had a cheerful log fire. Agatha asked for a gin and tonic, saying that although she was driving, one wouldn't hurt. He found them a table near the fire and went to get her drink and a pint of beer for himself.

Before he sat down, he removed his coat. Agatha shrugged her own coat off, wishing, because she had been feeling so low, that she had not decided to wear old clothes. Her trousers were baggy at the knees.

"So," he said, "what are you detecting?"

Agatha thought guiltily of Molly Kite, no doubt wondering what had happened to her.

"I'm trying again," she said, "to find out who murdered these people in Winter Parva."

"Any leads?"

"Still a lot of dead ends."

"Tell me about it."

So Agatha did. When she had finished, he said, "You should be careful. If George Southern was murdered because he knew the identity of the man who killed Bert Simple and he thought you were getting close, he might kill you."

"Well, I'll need to find him before he finds me," said Agatha.

"I must be getting back," he said.

"Yes, your wife must be wondering what's happened to you," said Agatha.

"Like you, I'm divorced. I live with my son. I was lucky to get custody. Do you work on Saturdays?"

"Not often."

"Why don't you come and see the farm?"

"I'd like that."

"I'll give you directions."

Agatha wrote them down. She felt as if the long-awaited spring was blossoming inside her.

When he dropped her at the supermarket, she felt she would leave Molly Kite until later.

She forgot about the other men in her life and looked forward to Saturday. But some caution prompted her to call on her friend, Mrs. Bloxby, who had a good knowledge of people over quite a wide area.

But Mrs. Bloxby said she had never heard of Paul Newton, but that she would ask around. She looked unusually distracted so Agatha asked her if anything was bothering her.

"The bishop," said Mrs. Bloxby. "He's back on the attack. Alf, he says, must do more to attract young people to the church. We are to have a pop group next Sunday. They call themselves The Charistmatic Christians. I have heard them. They are very loud. So we're back to that same old business — Jesus is your pal. Clap happy. No grandeur. No real spiritual belief. Nothing to be scared of which means nothing to respect."

"I think that's silly," said Agatha, who

hated to see her friend worried. "I'll see what I can do. I mean, it'll drive away the regulars and no young person is going to bother coming."

"On the contrary, they have quite a following. I suppose I am being dreadfully old-fashioned. Don't worry. The bishop will soon turn his attention elsewhere. Besides, it's kind of you to suggest it, but there really is nothing you can do."

"One thing," said Agatha before she left, "if Charles or James wants to know where I am, don't tell them."

Saturday dawned, damp, cold and drizzly. Agatha wore a dark green cashmere trouser suit and moderately high-heeled boots. She wondered what it would be like to be a farmer's wife. It was a pity he had a son. Wrapped in a rosy dream where the son was saying, "Dad, it's time you put the past behind you and got married again," Agatha followed the directions to the farm.

When she arrived in the farmyard, Paul came out to meet her. He was wearing a checked shirt with the sleeves rolled up, exposing powerful arms.

"Come in and have a coffee," he said, "and meet Luke, my son."

Agatha followed him into an impeccably

clean kitchen. A tall young man with a thatch of black hair and who looked very much like his father rose as Agatha and Paul entered.

"This is my son," said Paul. "Luke, this is Mrs. Raisin."

"Agatha, please."

"Wouldn't dream of it," said Luke, rising to his feet. "I am never familiar with the aged."

"Luke! A word with you," said his father furiously.

They moved into another room. Agatha could hear raised voices but not what they were saying. What a bad beginning!

At last, Paul came back. "I'm sorry about that. My son is very possessive. Usually, it's the other way around. But we won't let it spoil our day. Tell you what, I'll put the coffee on and while it's percolating, I'll show you my Charolais. I'm very proud of them. They took first prize last year at the Moreton show."

He glanced down at Agatha's boots. "You'd better borrow a pair of Wellingtons."

"I'll be all right," said Agatha. "My heels aren't very high."

She followed him out of the farmhouse, across the yard, and to where a large barn stood. Agatha could feel the damp, clinging

151

drizzle playing havoc with her make-up. Paul unfastened the door of the barn. "Go and take a look," he said. "Aren't they beautiful?"

You can take the girl out of the city, but you can't take the city out of the girl, and city-born Agatha's bones were made of pavement. "What marvellous beasts!" she said, hoping she wasn't expected to get nearer to the great white animals. The only time Agatha felt comfortable with cattle was when they were neatly cut up into steaks.

At last, feeling his visitor had admired his prize cattle long enough, Paul led the way back to the farmhouse.

Clasping a mug of coffee, Agatha asked if he minded if she had a cigarette. "Go ahead," he said. "I'll have one myself."

Bless the man, thought Agatha, lighting up. I really must marry him.

At that moment, Mrs. Bloxby was facing Toni Gilmour. The vicar's wife was incapable of lying, but she said, "I cannot tell you where Mrs. Raisin is. She really did not want anyone to know."

"I've tried her mobile, but it's switched off," said Toni, "and I really think she'll want to hear my news."

Mrs. Bloxby remembered that she had

only been instructed not to tell Charles or James where Agatha was.

"Is it really important?" she asked.

"Very."

"Mrs. Raisin is visiting a farmer called Paul Newton. I know his farm is in the Mircester area but that's all."

Agatha was back in the farm kitchen, feeling tired and miserable. Her boots were muddy and the rain had suddenly changed from a drizzle to a downpour, washing off what was left of her make-up. She felt she had walked miles and miles, looking at rain-sodden fields lying under a lowering sky.

Luke crashed into the kitchen. "Sit down," ordered his father. "I'm just about to serve lunch."

Shrugging on his coat, Luke said, "I'm going to the pub."

"I'm sorry about my son's manners," said Paul as the farm door slammed behind Luke.

But the door crashed open again. "Dad!" cried Luke. "Someone absolutely gorgeous has just driven up."

There came a tentative knock at the open door and then Toni walked in. She was wearing a long scarlet padded coat and her blond hair was tied up on top of her head.

"I'm sorry to butt in, Agatha," she said. "But I felt the news couldn't wait."

"This is my assistant, Toni Gilmour," said Agatha. "Toni, Paul Newton and his son, Luke."

"We were just about to have lunch," said Paul. "Do stay and join us, Miss Gilmour. My son is just leaving so you can have his meal."

"Actually, it's too wet out," said Luke. "I've decided to stay."

Paul switched off the gas on the cooker. "Luke, let's leave Agatha to have a private talk."

When they walked into the other room, Agatha said, "What's so steaming important that it couldn't wait? Snakes and bastards! What a day!"

"It's just this," said Toni, sitting down beside Agatha. She handed her a newspaper cutting. "This was in the morning's paper."

Agatha grabbed the paper and began to read. Then she let out a low whistle and briefly forgot about Paul. The announcement in the paper was that Gwen and John were engaged to be married.

"A concrete motive at last," said Agatha.

"I wondered if you would like me to go and see John Hale. I can catch him in his dressing room before tonight's show. I'll be tactful."

"Good idea."

Toni grinned. "I won't stay for lunch. Is this the latest?"

"I thought so," said Agatha, "but I'm beginning to think I loathe farms. Anyway, I wish I could get rid of the son."

Toni went to the door of the other room and called, "Goodbye."

Luke came shooting out. "Can't you stay?"

"Got to go."

"I was going to go to the pub. Why don't we both go and leave the olds alone?"

"All right," said Toni as Paul walked back into the kitchen. "I'll call you, Agatha, and let you know how I get on."

When they had left, Paul asked what it was all about, serving up a lunch of roast chicken while Agatha gave him the news.

After lunch, Agatha asked if she could use the bathroom and he showed her upstairs to a large one off what he said was his bedroom.

Feeling better after carefully repairing her make-up and brushing her hair until it shone, Agatha left the bathroom and was immediately seized in Paul's arms.

He kissed her so passionately that Agatha responded until she felt a warning bell at the back of her brain and pulled free.

"That was sudden," she said breathlessly.

"I'm sorry," he said. "I got carried away. Let's take things slowly then."

Does this farm need money? jeered a nasty little voice in Agatha's head.

She threw a nervous look at the bed. "Let's go back to the kitchen," she said.

They had only drunk mineral water with their meal. To Agatha's relief, Paul suggested they have brandy. I hope I'm not becoming a drunk, thought Agatha, but I feel I've had a shock.

"I didn't know you fancied me that much," she said.

"I do. Very much," said Paul. "When you've finished your brandy, why don't you go home and think things over? If you want to see me again, phone me."

Agatha let herself into her cottage. A lazy voice from her living room called, "In here."

Charles, thought Agatha. Why would he have to turn up this day of all days? I need to think.

Charles was lying on the sofa with the cats on his lap. He sat up, dislodging the cats, and surveyed Agatha.

"You look all mussed up," he said. "Been round a farm?"

"What makes you say that?"

156

"Your boots are caked in mud."

"I went for a walk across the fields." Agatha sat down in an armchair and pulled off her boots.

"I don't believe you," said Charles.

"I was detecting."

"You've got that old look in your eyes. What's his name?"

"Really, Charles. We're not married so you have no right to fire questions at me. There is some news about the case. John Hale is to marry Gwen Simple. Now, there's a motive. Toni is going to talk to him. He may be our murderer."

"In which case, young Toni should not be going near him."

"She'll be all right. She's seeing him at the theatre."

Toni made her way up to the dressing rooms that evening carrying a bouquet of flowers which she had told the stage door keeper she was delivering from a local florist. As she went, she wondered whether she had been wise to accept an invitation from Luke to visit a pop concert later that evening. He said he would pick her up at the stage door in half an hour's time. Toni knew that Agatha seemed to have found a new beau and might regard her date with the son as poaching on her territory. She hesitated outside a dressing room door with a gold star on it. It could be Gwen's. Then she heard a masculine voice singing, "Me, me, me," knocked on the door, and without waiting for a reply, she entered.

John was sitting in front of a mirror. He saw Toni in the mirror and said, "Just put them down anywhere. I'll find a vase for them later."

"I'm actually a private detective, working for Agatha Raisin," said Toni. "Here is my card. Only a few questions."

Had Toni not been so very pretty, John would have been angry, but he gave her an indulgent smile and said, "Pull up a chair and fire away."

Toni sat down on a little gilt chair. John was dressed in costume for the current production of *The Gondoliers.* He continued to apply his make-up.

"I see you are to marry Gwen Simple," said Toni.

"Yes, I am a lucky man, but what's that got to do with anything?"

"It seems so soon after the murder of her husband."

"I see what you're after. Well, I'm due on stage, so you can wait here and I'll have some words with you, young lady, after the first act." He threw down the towel he had wrapped round his neck, went swiftly to the door, went out, and Toni could hear the key turning in the lock.

What on earth do I do now? wondered Toni. She went over to the door and tugged at it. Should she stand up Luke and wait until the possible murderer came back?

She decided that it would be better to escape. There was a stage sword propped in one corner, not the *Mikado*'s sword, but a metal one with a dull edge.

She inserted the point of the sword in the door jamb, just at the lock, and using it like a crow bar, she wrenched it to one side. There was a splintering sound and the door sprang open.

Toni hurried out of the theatre, relieved to see Luke was early and was waiting for her.

When she got into his car, she said, "I've got to phone Agatha."

She told Agatha what had happened. "I'll go over in time for the end of the performance and ask him what the hell he was playing at," said Agatha.

When Toni rang off, Luke said, "She should never have sent a young girl like you. I thought she was an old toughie and she's after my father."

"If you are going to criticise Agatha then you can drop me off now," said Toni.

"Sorry. I just don't want Dad to make a mistake."

Agatha and Charles drove to the theatre in time for the end of the performance. The stage door keeper was on the phone and did not stop them as they hurried past. "The door is broken open so it should be easy to find him," said Agatha.

They located the dressing room and walked in. Faintly they could hear sounds of applause. At last they heard people coming along to the dressing rooms. The door opened and John walked in.

"What the hell are you doing here?" he demanded.

"Accusing you of kidnapping for a start," said Agatha. "What do you think you were doing, locking my assistant in here?"

"I hadn't time to talk to her," he said sulkily. "Say what you want and get out."

He sat down in front of the mirror and began to take off his make-up.

"You are to marry Gwen Simple," said Agatha.

"So what?"

"Rather soon after her husband was murdered, don't you think?"

"I love Gwen and she loves me. Why should we wait?"

"It gives you a motive to have murdered Bert Simple."

"Get out. You're not the police and you have no right to question me."

"Call them," said Agatha, "and explain to them why you locked up Toni Gilmour."

"I was about to go on stage," he said defiantly. "I was stressed. The police will understand. She was here under false pretences. She claimed to be delivering flowers from a florist. Now, get out."

"Come on, Aggie," said Charles.

Agatha moved towards the door. "Does Gwen know you are after her money?" she asked.

The flowers Toni had brought had been put in a vase. John seized the vase and hurled it at Agatha. She jumped to the side and the glass vase hit the door and shattered.

"Nasty temper you've got," said Charles. "Let's get out of here."

Toni enjoyed her evening with Luke but said cautiously she would let him know about a future date. He had made a few more caustic remarks about Agatha during the evening. Toni had responded by saying that

161

most men found Agatha attractive.

She decided to have a talk to Agatha in the office on Monday and find out whether her boss was really serious about Paul Newton.

The following day when Agatha appeared in the kitchen, Charles asked, "Why are you all dressed up?"

"I'm going to church. Mrs. Bloxby needs my moral support."

Charles burst out laughing. "From you?"

"Yes, from me. The poxy bishop has wished a pop group on the vicar. She is upset."

"This I must see," said Charles. "I'll come with you."

The old church was full. There was an audience of young people and thin, avid-looking bespectacled women.

Hymns were sung while the new audience shifted restlessly. Then Alf Bloxby, tall, grey-haired and scholarly, introduced The Charismatic Christians.

They started to play and sing, electric guitars magnified to an ear-splitting pitch.

They began to sing: "Jesus is my buddy / He walks along wi' me / In the pub and at the gig / It's where he'll always be."

The thin women waved their arms in the air. The audience of young people waved their arms as well.

"Where are you going?" yelled Charles, as Agatha got to her feet.

"Wait and see," said Agatha.

She went out of the church, entered by a side door and went down to the crypt. She found the switchboard and shut off the electricity. She saw keys hanging up on a board by the door. She found the one for the crypt door and left, locking it behind her and taking the key.

Upstairs, Charles thought, Agatha's done it now.

At first the band seemed unaware their sound system had been switched off. Their voices were faint and reedy. Someone at the back of the church began to boo. The band stopped playing and stared at each other.

Rising to the occasion, Alf announced the next hymn. The congregation sang, "There Is a Green Hill Far Away," while a flustered verger appeared and spoke to the band, who began to pack up their instruments.

Standing outside, Agatha waited until she saw them getting into their van and driving off. Then she went down to the crypt again, unlocked the door and replaced the key.

She waited outside the church until the

congregation came out. Mrs. Bloxby came up to her, looking worried. "You really shouldn't have done such a thing, Mrs. Raisin," she said. "It must have been you. Alf is upset. He had come round to the idea and was enjoying preaching to a full church."

Mrs. Bloxby was accosted by a parishioner. Charles, who had heard what she had said, comforted Agatha by saying, "Stick to detective work, Aggie. No good deed goes unpunished. Cheer up. That band really was awful. Alf Bloxby seems to be getting it in the neck."

As the vicar stood at the entrance to the church, an elderly gentleman could be heard berating him. "A disgrace," he yelled. "Sacrilege! How dare you let such freaks invade the sanctity of the church!"

"He's going to wake up to the fact that if he goes on being trendy, he'll lose his regulars," said Charles. "Got any more detecting to take your mind off it?"

"One thing," said Agatha. "I never got around to interviewing Molly Kite, the girl who worked for George."

"Okay. Let's go. We'll get something to eat in a pub on the way."

Molly Kite was at home and ushered them

into an unsavoury dark living room. The air was full of the smells of old booze and cigarette smoke. Five cats prowled around the room over the stained and battered furniture. Her father was slumped in an armchair in front of the television set, snoring loudly.

"Why don't we all go to the pub for a drink?" suggested Agatha, feeling she could not bear to wait a moment longer in such a room.

"Great," said Molly. "I'll get my coat."

Five minutes later they were seated at a pub in the high street. Molly ordered a double vodka and Red Bull, downed it and asked for another.

"What we want to know is do you know if George Southern was trying to blackmail someone," said Agatha.

Molly's large brown eyes widened. Her make-up was smudged and black circles of mascara were under her eyes. Agatha guessed she had not taken off her make-up from the night before. Despite the cold of the day, she was wearing a flimsy blouse and torn jeans under a thin wool coat.

"If he was, he didn't say nothing to me," she said.

"Did he say anything about coming into money?" pursued Agatha.

"Well, he started reading travel brochures and saying he was sick o' the village and wanted to get out. The shop never made much money. Load o' tat, if you ask me. The police asked me about money. They searched the place. My cousin what's in the police, he says, like, they looked at his bank accounts and apart from one thousand pounds, there was nothing else odd there. George was always beefing on about not having money and that the shop would be repossessed."

"Who inherited?" asked Charles.

"Some poor bugger o' a nephew down in Devon. Was cursing about all the debts, he was."

"But do you think that George believed he would soon have money?" asked Agatha.

"Well, not 'zactly. But he started singing and chuckling and saying how he would soon be made for life."

"Do you think he knew the identity of the murderer?" asked Charles.

"Maybe. Suppose so. Guess that's what got him killed."

"So who in this village has enough money to set George up for life?" asked Agatha.

"Dunno. Maybe the blacksmith. Bit of a miser. His uncle owned a pub over Ancombe way and died and left it to him. He sold it to a brewery."

They could get nothing more of interest out of Molly. After they had dropped her off at her house, Charles said, "It does look as if the blacksmith is the one. He had the money. He built the trap. He sharpened the sword. Let's go and see him."

"He'll just shout and threaten us," protested Agatha. "He's a beast."

"Nonetheless, let's go and rattle his cage."

But the smithy was empty. A cold wind moaned through the pieces of wrought iron that littered the yard.

"Let's try the house," said Charles. Agatha followed reluctantly.

"I only hope she doesn't throw something at me," she said.

Charles knocked at the battered door of the redbrick house. A curtain twitched and then the door opened. Mrs. Crosswith was wearing a smart blue wool dress and high heels.

"We would like to speak to your husband," said Agatha.

"Ain't here."

"Where is he?"

"Bangkok."

"Why?"

"Holiday and I hopes he stays there

forever. Now, sod off!"

The door was slammed in their faces.

"Well, that's that," said Charles.

"No, it isn't." Agatha scowled. "Usually she looks like a bag lady. I think she's expecting someone. Let's wait at the end of the lane in the car."

"This is boring," said Charles, after ten minutes.

"Wait. This is all part of detecting."

"Yawn."

A car turned into the lane. "That's it!" said Agatha. "Let's see who it is."

They drove up the lane, parked round the corner from the house. Agatha jumped out followed by Charles. They looked round the corner just in time to see Mrs. Crosswith enfolded in the passionate embrace of a large burly man in overalls. Then they moved indoors.

Agatha and Charles got back in the car. "Let's hope the blacksmith doesn't come back suddenly or there will be another murder," said Agatha.

Charles left later that day, leaving Agatha to face a lonely evening. She was just putting Mama Livia's lasagne into the microwave when her phone rang.

It was Paul Newton. "Have you had dinner yet?" he asked.

"Not yet."

"How about meeting me at Russell's in Broadway in an hour's time."

"Great," said Agatha. "I'll be there."

When she rang off, she rushed for the stairs to get up to the bathroom to start preparing for her date and tripped over her cats. Cursing, she got to her feet. Hodge and Boswell mewed accusingly and Agatha realised she hadn't fed them. Although Agatha mostly lived on junk food, she wouldn't dream of giving her cats anything but fresh fish. It took time to prepare their meal and feed them.

Agatha hated being late so it was a flustered woman who arrived at Russell's. As she walked into the restaurant, she saw her reflection in a mirror behind the bar and realised she had forgotten to put lipstick on.

When Paul rose from a table to greet her, she brushed past him, saying, "Be with you in a minute."

In the ladies' room, she scrabbled in her handbag for a lipstick. The only one she could find was orange and she was wearing a red sweater. It would have to do. No way was she going out there with bare lips.

Paul got up again as she emerged. "Everything all right?" he asked.

"Oh, yes," said Agatha, giving him an orange smile.

They chose their meals and then Paul talked about farming while Agatha, not really listening, wondered if the blacksmith had gone on holiday or fled out of the country.

"It was terrible last year," Paul was saying. "My fields were flooded."

"How awful," murmured Agatha, thinking, I really should call on Bill Wong. He hasn't called me in ages.

She suddenly realised Paul was coming to the end of an anecdote. "And old Jimmy said, 'Reckon you do be right.' " Paul laughed heartily and Agatha laughed as well.

This won't do, she thought frantically. You can't have a marriage where you don't even listen to the man.

He then asked Agatha how work was going and Agatha chatted on until the end of the meal, thinking all the time, he's nice and strong and I haven't had sex in ages. But it's no go. There just isn't that spark there. She felt suddenly depressed and insisted on paying for the meal as a compensation for having encouraged him.

They were just getting up to leave when Luke, Paul's son, walked into the restaurant. "Hi, Pops!" he said, ignoring Agatha. "I thought you'd like a lift home. The police are out tonight with their breathalysers. I can run you back for your car in the morning."

"How did you know I was here?" demanded Paul.

"You told Jimmy where you were in case there was any trouble with the lambing," said Luke.

"And is there?"

"No, fortunately. Let's go."

"I'll see you outside," said Paul. "I want to say goodnight to Agatha."

When his son had left, Paul took her hand. "I can send him away," he said. "We could have a nightcap at your place."

"Maybe another time," said Agatha. "Got an early start in the morning."

This is silly, thought Agatha. Why must I chase after men I have nothing in common with? She let herself into her cottage. But it would be nice, she thought sadly, to have a warm man in a warm bed.

The next morning, she called at police headquarters and asked to speak to Bill Wong, only to be told it was his day off.

Agatha headed out to his home, dreading meeting Bill's mother, who, she knew, did not like her one bit. In fact, she often thought that Bill seemed unaware that his mother put a stop to him having any relationship with any woman whatsoever. His father was Hong Kong Chinese but had been in England for so long that he had a Gloucestershire accent.

Mrs. Wong answered the door. She was wearing an apron over a droopy dress and carpet slippers. The last woman alive to wear an apron, thought Agatha.

"You can't see him," she said. "Goodbye." The door slammed.

Agatha was retreating down the path when the door opened again and Bill called, "I thought I heard your voice. Come in. Poor mum has such a bad memory for faces that she did not recognise you and thought you were selling something."

Oh, yeah, thought Agatha, but followed him to his home and into the antiseptic living room where everything was so clean and polished that it glittered.

"You're supposed to take the plastic covering off the furniture," said Agatha. "Must be hell on the bum in the hot weather."

"Only if you sit on it naked," said Bill equably. "Mum says it keeps the dust off and we only use this room for guests. We can join her in the kitchen, if you like?"

"No, this is fine. I called on the blacksmith

yesterday only to find he's gone to Bangkok. Did you know about this?"

"No. We're still on the case, of course. But to be honest, we're not getting any further," said Bill. "Winter Parva is a small village. Someone must know something. What about Gareth Craven? He must know the villagers well."

"I'll try him again," said Agatha. "There's something else." She told Bill about Mrs. Crosswith's affair. "And," said Agatha, "I bet the new boyfriend turns out to like beating up women. Women like her never learn."

"We'd better get after Harry Crosswith," said Bill. "But the trouble is, we've got no evidence that he is a murderer."

"Did forensics not come up with anything?" asked Agatha.

"Not even a hair. The trouble is with all those reality crime shows on television, everyone who watches them gets instructions on how to clean up a crime scene. There was no forced entry. You and Lacey just walked in. Somebody took that sword out of the theatre. Maybe Southern himself, planning some other joke."

"How did you get on with Gwen Simple?" asked Agatha.

"I think she helped as much as she could."

"And the son?"

"Him, too. The latest news is that they're going to sell the bakery."

"John Hale will like that," said Agatha. "He's desperate for money."

"He may be disappointed. Gwen gave the shop to her son so any money from the sale goes to him."

Agatha grinned. "Then I'll be amazed if the wedding goes ahead."

"I often wonder about Hale," said Bill. "Rumour round the village says that he was keen on Gwen for a long time."

"So was Gareth Craven. I still wonder if he hired me to investigate so that he wouldn't be suspected. I think I'll pay him a visit, although I am wasting precious time. I told him I wouldn't charge him until I had something concrete."

"So how's your love life?" asked Bill.

"Know anything about a farmer called Paul Newton?"

"Rings a bell. I know, he reported the theft of a tractor last year and I went out to take down the details. Seems pleasant. Been courting you?"

"I suppose you could call it that. I think he just wants sex."

"How did you meet him?"

"He came up to me in Jacey's. Said he was a friend of James."

"So ask James about him."

"James is away on his travels," said Agatha.

"I haven't offered you coffee or anything," said Bill. "I'll ask Mother to make us some."

"No, don't!" said Agatha. "I'd better be off. I'll call on Gareth and then get back to all the work I ought to be doing."

Gareth seemed pleased to see Agatha. He supplied her with a cup of excellent coffee and an ashtray.

"Any news?" he asked.

"Dead ends all round except that Harry Crosswith has gone to Bangkok and his wife is having an affair."

"She'd never dare!"

"I assure you, she has. I saw them."

"What did the man look like?"

"Big, heavyset chap, working clothes, curly brown hair, broad piggy face."

"That sounds like Jed Widdle."

"Who's he?"

"He's a builder. Works on construction sites. Lives in a cottage on the road out of the village. I wouldn't have thought she would have had the courage. And I don't care if Harry is in Bangkok. He'd need to be dead before she started anything."

Agatha looked at him and then said slowly,

"What if he is dead?"

"Not another murder!"

"I'd like to check. I'll get someone to help me."

Agatha phoned Simon and told him to join her outside the market hall. When he finally arrived, she briefed him, and then said, "Where would they have got rid of a body?"

"It's a smithy, isn't it?" said Simon. "Cut him up and put him in the fire."

"We'll park down the lane from the smithy," said Agatha. "We wait until she goes out and then we start to search."

He got into Agatha's car and they drove to the end of the lane.

"Will spring never come?" mourned Simon, looking out at the grey day. Although there was no rain, the wind was rising. A crisp packet flattened itself against the windscreen before being torn away to dance up the lane.

"Does Toni ever talk about me?" asked Simon.

Agatha glanced sideways at his sad jester's face. "I'm afraid not, Simon. Give up. I don't think she'll ever forgive you for dumping that girl at the altar. You couldn't have been that keen on Toni to go and propose to someone else, and then decide you didn't want her."

"It all happened when I was in the army in Afghanistan," said Simon sulkily. "You bond with the oddest people out there."

"Get down!" said Agatha. "Here she comes."

Mrs. Crosswith was coming down the lane. She was wearing high-heeled boots and a scarlet coat.

"Right," said Agatha, straightening up. "Let's go and have a look."

"That's odd," said Simon as they walked into the yard.

"What's odd?"

"The smithy isn't locked and there's all this metal lying around. It's a wonder thieves haven't pinched it and shipped it to China."

They walked into the smithy. "It's pretty dark in here," said Simon. "Want me to switch on the lights?"

"No, leave it," said Agatha. "Don't want to draw attention to ourselves."

"It's an earth floor," said Simon. "Handy for burying a body. Hey! What's this?"

Agatha came to join him. "What's what?"

"Look where the earth has been freshly turned over. Give me something to dig with."

Agatha found a spade and handed it to

him. "Go carefully," she warned. "If there's a body there, we don't want to be accused of messing up a crime scene."

Simon scraped away at the earth with the back of the spade. "Oh!" he exclaimed. "Bones."

"Can't be the blacksmith. There would be a decomposing body at least."

"They could have boiled the flesh off."

"Ugh! Leave it. Let's get out of here and I'll call the police."

Agatha and Simon stood and shivered in the cold while a forensics team worked on the floor of the smithy.

Then there was a shriek of outrage as Mrs. Crosswith ran into the yard. "What the hell are you doing?" she screamed.

Inspector Wilkes said solemnly, "We need to take you in for questioning. A skeleton has been found buried in the smithy."

"That's Jess, you idiot," she shouted.

"Jess?"

"Our old dog."

Wilkes turned a fulminating eye on Agatha before striding into the smithy.

With a sinking heart, Agatha waited for him to reappear while Mrs. Crosswith said to her, "If it was you, mucking around in there and poking your nose in, I'll have you for trespass."

When Wilkes came out, he said, "I am sorry to have troubled you, Mrs. Crosswith. But you will need to come to headquarters with us. We have some questions to ask you about the whereabouts of your husband."

Bill must have told him about Bangkok, thought Agatha. "And you," said Wilkes to Agatha, "follow us. I've got some questions to ask you."

Agatha waited a long time with Simon at police headquarters in Mircester until they were summoned to an interviewing room. Wilkes was flanked by a detective Agatha had not met before.

The interview began. "Why were you searching around the smithy?" began Wilkes.

So Agatha told him of her suspicions.

"Did you tell Detective Wong that you meant to go and search the smithy?"

"Definitely not. When did Harry Crosswith leave for Bangkok?"

"Just leave the investigation to the police," snapped Wilkes. "I will not charge you with wasting police time on this occasion, but a repeat of anything like this and I will throw the book at you."

When they finally left police headquarters,

Simon said, "They'll check all the airlines and if there is no sign of the blacksmith having booked a flight, then that wife of his will be in trouble."

They went back to the office and, to Simon's dismay, he was given the details of two missing dogs and told to look for them.

Simon often wanted to shine in Agatha's eyes. He knew she rated him much lower than Toni and when she went on holiday, it was Toni who was left in charge.

To his relief, he found both dogs at the Animal Rescue Centre, and wondered why the owners never thought to check there first. Also as both dogs had been microchipped and the owners had been informed and were on their way to collect their pets, it cancelled out the agency's fee.

He suddenly decided to go back to the smithy and see if he could find anything. It was getting dark and he figured he could hide in some bushes he had seen at the entrance to the blacksmith's yard. But the smithy was dark and deserted. He went round to the back and saw the redbrick house. A light was on in a downstairs room. Simon crept up to the window and listened.

"Don't worry, my chuck, they'll never find the bastard," said a man's voice.

"There hasn't been rain in ages. What if

that pond dries up?"

"It's been too grey and cold. No sun. Stop . . ."

The voices moved away and the light in the downstairs room went off. The front door began to open. Simon nipped quietly round the side of the building, his heart hammering.

He waited until they had driven off and wondered what to do. He couldn't phone the police, because he and Agatha had been warned off.

What pond?

He took himself off to the pub, ordered a half of lager, and said to the barmaid, "Are there any ponds around the village?"

"Thinking of going fishing?" she asked.

"Something like that."

"Won't do you no good, m'dear. There's just the one pond up on Sar Field and it got nothing in there but rubbish."

"And how do I get to Sar Field?"

"You go out the village, past the church and just before the turn-off to the Evesham road, you'll see the pond in the field on your right. But what do you want to go there for?"

"It's for a bet," said Simon.

He gulped down his drink and left. He blessed the day he had taken up fishing, because he had a pair of waders in the back of his car.

Simon located the pond and walked towards it carrying a torch and his waders. He sat down on a tussock of grass and pulled his waders on. He stood up and shone his torch at the pond. A shopping market trolley stuck out at the edge of the water along with an old sofa. Wishing he had brought a stick to test the depth of the water, he gingerly stepped into the pond.

A sliver of new moon shone down. Icy ripples ran across the pond, driven by a stiff wind. He shone his powerful torch down into the water but the ripples distorted everything.

It was a quiet night in the pub and the barmaid was telling everyone about the young man who was going to the pond for a bet. Jed Widdle heard her and made for the door.

Two young men finished their drinks and one said, "Let's go to the pond. I want to see what this bet is."

Simon was beginning to feel it was all hopeless. He would need a long rod to poke about. He had just reached the edge of the pond when a pair of strong hands seized him and thrust him down into the icy water. He fought and struggled, feeling himself getting weaker, when he was suddenly released. His attacker had propelled him into a deep part of the pond. He struggled to the shore, cursing the dragging weight of his water-filled waders.

The two young men from the pub helped him out. "What's going on, mate?" one asked. "We saw Jed Widdle trying to drown you."

"Get the police," said Simon.

Wrapped in blankets, Simon sat in a police car. Detective Constable Alice Peterson was in the front. "Can I borrow your phone?" asked Simon. "Mine's at the bottom of the pond. I have to phone Agatha."

"Sorry," said Alice. "Wilkes would kill me."

The ringing of her bedside phone woke Agatha. "What is it?" she demanded.

"It's Chris Jenty here, Agatha. *Mircester Echo*. Do you know what's going on at the pond outside Winter Parva? Your detective is there in a police car. Someone tried to attack him and the police are draining the pond."

By the time Agatha arrived at the pond, a

small crowd of villagers had gathered. She saw Simon sitting in the police car and rapped on the window. He rolled it down.

"Are you all right?" asked Agatha. "Are they looking for Crosswith?"

"I think he must be in the pond," said Simon. "I was looking because I overheard Mrs. Crosswith and Jed talking about a pond."

"That's enough, Mrs. Raisin," said Alice. "Mr. Black will be questioned later."

Police had put tape around the scene, which Agatha had ducked under on her arrival. A policeman told her to get back and she reluctantly agreed.

Chris Jenty came to join her. "I heard Wilkes order a search for Jed Widdle. He took off over the fields, say the fellows who rescued Simon. Jed was trying to drown him. I heard Wilkes say that if the body of the blacksmith is found, he'll forgive Simon. If not, he'll throw the book at him for interfering in a police investigation."

"Rubbish," said Agatha. "Oh, look. A couple of divers have arrived. I didn't think the pond would be that deep."

"Maybe not. But it's a bit of a rubbish tip and they've got to scrabble around the bottom."

A couple of floodlights had been erected.

Agatha nervously lit a cigarette. "Disgusting habit," complained a man behind her.

Agatha swung round. "Oh, shut up, you tiresome man," she yelled.

"Steady," admonished Chris. "Look."

One of the divers had surfaced and held up a hand.

"If they've found a body and it's weighted down, how are they going to get it out?" asked Agatha.

"Pull it out," said Chris. "They're fastening a rope to the tow bar of that police Land Rover."

Everyone fell silent. The Land Rover backed slowly. Something wrapped in black plastic was slowly pulled up from the pond and onto the bank. A tent was quickly erected over it.

Patrick Mulligan appeared at Agatha's side. "I got a tipoff," he said. "I went to the smithy. Police all over the place but no sign of the wife."

"Anyone in the police here that you know?" asked Agatha.

"Bill Wong's just turned up."

"He won't dare to speak to either of us with the police around," said Patrick. "But I recognise that sergeant over there. I'll have a quick word."

He ducked under the tape. Agatha shivered and waited.

Patrick eventually came back. "He says it looks like Jed and the wife were stopped in their car on the Mircester road."

"Think they did all the murders?" asked Chris.

"Can't think why," said Patrick. "Why don't you go home, Agatha? I'll wait here and phone you with any news."

But Agatha had just seen Simon being driven off.

"I'll go to police headquarters and wait for Simon."

When she sat in the reception area at police headquarters, Agatha was joined by Toni. "Patrick phoned me," she said. "I came to see if Simon was all right."

"I think so. He must have had a bad shock," said Agatha. "He should really go to hospital for a tetanus shot. That pond was filthy. I'm angry with him."

"Why?" demanded Toni. "If it hadn't been for him, maybe they'd never have found the body."

"Maybe." Agatha stifled a yawn. She took a pocket mirror out of her bag and looked at her face. She had pouches under her eyes and lines of fatigue down either side of her mouth. The youth and beauty that was Toni glowed beside her.

I wish a fairy would wave a magic wand and let me look like her for just one day, thought Agatha.

Simon emerged, wearing a grey track suit, much too big for him and with the trousers rolled up at the bottom. "Oh, Toni," he said, ignoring Agatha, "how great of you to come."

"Where are your own clothes?" asked Toni.

"They kept them in case I shoved the blacksmith in the pond myself. They're just being nasty, because he was probably down there for weeks."

"Have you had a tetanus shot?" asked Agatha.

"Yes, the police doctor gave me a checkup as well. You know, Toni, I would love a good cup of coffee. Is there somewhere we can go?"

"Nowhere open this early," said Agatha. "I am here as well as Toni, you know. Let's go to the office and have coffee and you can tell us all about it."

In the office, Simon clutched a mug of coffee and described his adventures.

"You should have told me what you were doing," admonished Agatha. "On the other hand, the police should be grateful. They'd never have got on to it if you hadn't investigated. Well done!"

"You would think I had killed the man myself the way they went on," said Simon. He stifled a yawn.

"Get home to bed and don't bother coming in today," ordered Agatha.

"Do you want me to answer these phones?" asked Toni.

"Let them ring," said Agatha. "I'll prepare a statement and make sure everyone knows Simon is the hero of the day."

When Simon had left, Agatha typed out a statement and handed it to Toni, who began to answer the phones and read it out.

Patrick Mulligan appeared an hour later. "They charged Jed Widdle with the murder of the blacksmith."

"That was quick," exclaimed Agatha. "Surely it will take them a few days to find forensic proof."

"You'll never believe this," said Patrick. "When the silly ass was wrapping up the body and putting rocks in the bag, he dropped in his driving license at the same time. Wilkes is charging him with the other murders."

"He can't have any proof."

"Well, the police got a bruising in the press over the unsolved murders and they're determined to get him to cough to them. He may admit to it."

"Why on earth?"

"It seems Jed is deeply in love with Mrs. Crosswith. They're persuading him that if he admits to all the murders, they won't charge her with anything."

"That's nasty. How did you hear all this?"

"I went to the police canteen and heard all the gossip. They sometimes forget I'm not a member of the force anymore."

"Roy Silver is on the phone," said Toni.

"Tell him I'll call him later." Poor Roy, thought Agatha. He must be furious at having missed out. "Go home, Patrick," said Agatha. "I'm going to get some sleep later."

"Go home now," said Toni. "I'm not a bit tired. I can run things with Phil and Mrs. Freedman."

Chapter Seven

Agatha wearily let herself into her cottage. The phone started to ring. She had recently changed to an ex-directory number so she felt safe to answer it.

It was Paul Newton. "I thought you might be at home. I've been watching events on television. Are you all right?"

"Just tired."

"Want to meet up for a meal later and tell me about it?"

Agatha hesitated for a moment. Then she said, "It's my time to treat you. I'll meet you in the Black Bear in Moreton-in-Marsh at seven."

"That's great. See you then."

Just as she put down the receiver, the phone rang again. It was Charles. "Hullo, Agatha," he said.

"Goodbye, Charles," retorted Agatha and hung up. She had suddenly decided she was fed up with Charles treating her in his usual cavalier way. Maybe she didn't fancy Paul, but an evening with a man who admired her was preferable to the company of Charles who too often looked on her with a cynical eye.

Contrary to her usual behaviour when out on a date, Agatha arrived at the Black Bear wearing comfortable clothes and the minimum of make-up.

Paul rose and kissed her on the cheek.

Why! He's rather what I would call husky, thought Agatha, coming to the opinion that she had previously formed too harsh an opinion of him.

After they had ordered their food — steak pie and chips for both of them — Paul asked Agatha about the latest murder and Agatha was glad to talk it over to an appreciative listener.

When she had finished, Paul leaned across the table and took her hand. "It's a dangerous job. Have you ever considered giving it up?"

"I don't think I would be good at anything else," said Agatha, "except my old job of public relations and I did get really tired of that."

"Never think of getting married again?"

"After two marriages which didn't work

out," said Agatha, gently removing her hand, "I'm a bit wary of the idea."

Toni received a phone call from Luke. "My dad's gone out for the evening."

"Doesn't he usually?"

"No. Is he seeing your boss?"

"I wouldn't know," said Toni. "Why?"

"Oh, nothing. Feel like going to a movie tomorrow?"

Toni hesitated. She liked him but not that much. "This latest murder means we are all working overtime," she said. "I'll phone you."

Paul was saying, "I thought all women dreamed of marriage. No responsibilities. Have some loving man to look after them."

"Well, that's only a dream," said Agatha cynically. "The reality is different."

Paul's phone rang.

He listened and said impatiently, "Okay. I'm coming." He rang off and said to Agatha, "There's trouble with the lambing. I've got to go. Luke sounds frantic. Do you want to come with me?"

"I'm still tired. Off you go. I'll get this. It's my turn."

As she watched him leave, Agatha felt her

waistband tightening. Why did I eat all that steak pie? she mourned.

She asked for coffee and then fell into a dream of being a farmer's wife, which had more to do with Hollywood and cheap romances than reality.

But reality in the form of Charles Fraith came into the restaurant. "I drove over to see what you were in such a snit about," he said, sitting down opposite. He looked at Paul's empty plate. "You've been on a date and he left."

"It was Paul Newton."

"Who's Paul Newton?" asked Charles.

"Just someone who wants to marry me."

"Why?"

"What an insulting thing to ask."

"Your track record with men has been awful," said Charles.

"You included," snapped Agatha.

He gave a little shrug. Charles was like her cats, thought Agatha angrily. Doling out affection when it suited him and dropping in and out of her life like a cat using a cat flap on the door.

"So what's all this about the latest murder?" asked Charles.

Agatha told him the latest news, feeling herself beginning to relax. Charles was a good listener.

When she had finished, Charles said, "I often feel sorry for young Simon. You don't seem to rate him much, but he does have a way of finding out things. And do you think Jed Widdle will confess to all the murders to save Mrs. Crosswith?"

"Seems to be possible."

"But could it be true?"

"I don't know. But the police have been under pressure so they'll want it to be true. Jed Widdle won't be able to afford a very good lawyer. I mean, a good lawyer could make mincemeat of the case against him for the first two murders. No actual proof. But no one approached Jed for an alibi because he was never even suspected."

"Don't you want to give up?" asked Charles. "I mean, it's dragged on so long that even if Jed didn't commit the earlier murders, I don't see you finding out anything now."

"It's tempting," said Agatha. "I may get married and be a lady of leisure."

"To this Paul Newton? What does he do?"

"He's a farmer."

"Oh, come on, Aggie. See yourself as a farmer's wife?"

"Why not?" said Agatha sulkily.

"Is he a toy boy?"

"No, he's about my age."

Said Charles, "If he hasn't been married before, be careful."

"He has," said Agatha. "And he has a grown-up son."

"And what does the son think of his future stepmother?"

"For heaven's sakes, Charles. I've only had a few dates. His son phoned this evening. Something's up with the lambing."

"Ah, I can see you out in the field in the driving rain with mud on your boots, Agatha. A real daughter of the soil."

"Oh, do shut up. I'm going home. I'm tired."

It was a particularly dreary next few days for Agatha. She had to deal with two nasty divorce cases which involved a lot of standing around in freezing weather while Phil took photographs for evidence. Divorce cases always made Agatha feel grubby. Her thoughts kept turning to Paul Newton's well-appointed farmhouse and the security of marriage.

He sent her flowers and phoned her, saying he couldn't wait to see her again.

By the week-end, she caved in and went out on another date with him. She talked to Paul a lot about her life and about her previous marriage to James Lacey.

"So I'm the only man in your life?" asked Paul.

"I do have men friends, Detective Bill Wong and Charles Fraith, but no one serious."

"Did you say Charles Fraith? Sir Charles Fraith?"

"Yes. Why?"

"There was something in *The Times* this morning. I've got a copy in my briefcase." He fished out the paper and turned to the social columns. "Here it is. You'll know all about it, of course."

Agatha read that Charles was engaged to a Caroline Featherington. She felt as if she had been punched in the stomach. Why had he said nothing to her?

"You look surprised," said Paul.

"I knew he was planning on proposing," lied Agatha. "I didn't expect him to pop the question so soon."

"I was going to wait," said Paul, "but your friend's engagement has given me courage." He brought a small jewel box out of his pocket. He handed it to her. "What about it, Agatha?"

Agatha opened the box. She was aware of the eyes of the other diners about them fastened on her. A solitaire diamond ring flashed and sparkled in the candlelight on their table.

All Agatha suddenly saw, looking at that ring, was an antidote to the long, single years ahead. No more visits from Charles. No more holidays with feckless, faithless Charles.

"Thank you," she said and put the ring on her engagement finger as the people at the table next to theirs began to clap. Paul called for champagne.

"What does Luke think about this?" asked Agatha.

"I haven't told him yet, but he'll be pleased."

After a night of rumbustious sex, Agatha appeared in the office to tell the staff of her forthcoming wedding. They all clustered around to admire the ring. "I see Charles is getting married as well," said Toni.

"Is he?" said Agatha casually. "Good for him."

Toni covertly studied Agatha's face. She had seen Agatha in love before and Agatha did not seem to have the same happiness or elation that she had had then. Worse than that, Toni had received a phone call early on in the morning from a furious Luke, saying he would do anything to stop the marriage. Ought she to warn Agatha? Better not. Agatha would find out about Luke's disapproval soon enough.

But in the following weeks, Agatha did not find out. Luke was not exactly friendly and seemed to make a point of going out whenever she arrived at the farmhouse, but he had given her his congratulations.

As for Agatha, she acted her new role as countrywoman with enthusiasm, even going so far as to take cookery lessons from Mrs. Bloxby. Her very acting served to remove her from reality and make her feel comfortable and useful. She forgot about the murders and the fact that Jed had, in her opinion, been wrongly charged with the three of them. Charles had not rung or called.

One Saturday, the phone rang. Luke answered it. When he rang off, he said, "That was the police, Dad. They think they've found that tractor of yours and want you to go to police headquarters."

"I'll go right away. Coming, Agatha?"

"It's all right," said Luke. "You go. I'll look after Agatha. Time I got to know my future stepmother better."

"That's the stuff," said Paul. "Back soon."

■ ■ ■ ■

When Paul had left, Luke said, "I'd like to show you the latest arrival. The prettiest little ram you've ever seen."

"Right you are," said Agatha, glad the young man was being friendly at last. She pulled on a serviceable pair of rubber boots and put on her Barbour.

Luke led the way across the fields. The day was cold and spots of rain were beginning to fall. "We're walking miles," complained Agatha at last.

"It's a big farm. You see that little stone building over there? That's where the ram is."

"Why isn't it with its mother?"

"It is." He swung up the door. "In you go."

Agatha peered into the gloom. Then she swung round in alarm as the door banged shut.

"What are you playing at?" she shouted.

"You can stay in there and rot unless you promise to break off your engagement to my dad," called Luke. "No one ever comes near here. You can shout your bloody head off. No one will hear you."

■ ■ ■ ■

Paul returned home to find a typewritten note on the kitchen table. He read: "Dear Paul, I am sorry I cannot go through with the marriage. Please forgive me, Agatha."

He ran upstairs to his son's room. "What's this?" he shouted at Luke, waving the note. "What happened to her? There was no call from police headquarters. It was a hoax. Where is she?"

"Said she was sick of it all and didn't want to face you," said Luke. "It never would have worked out."

Simon had managed to persuade Toni to join him for a drink. Like Charles, Toni felt sorry for Simon and thought Agatha might have given him better detecting jobs after he had found where the body in the pond was.

They had just started on their drinks when a red-faced young man approached their table. He looked down at Toni. "You Luke's girlfriend?" he asked.

"No," said Toni. "I know Luke, but I'm not his girlfriend."

"Pity. Someone should stop him."

"Doing what?" asked Toni.

"That woman his father's engaged to, he says he'll kill her rather than let his father marry her."

Toni and Simon exchanged startled looks. As the young man lumbered back to the bar, Toni said, "I think we'd better look for Agatha. She's probably out at that farmhouse."

"She can look after herself," said Simon, annoyed that this rare chance of being with Toni was being spoiled.

"You stay there if you like," said Toni. "I'm going."

"Oh, all right. But we're going to look silly," said Simon. "Did Agatha say where the farm was?"

"I've got the address and number," said Toni. "I've been there. It's not far."

Paul answered the door to them. "Is Agatha here?" asked Toni.

"She's left me," said Paul heavily. "Come in."

He led the way into the kitchen and showed them the note.

"Agatha would never do this!" said Toni. "Do you know your son has been threatening to kill her?"

"Rubbish!"

"Ask him!" said Toni.

Paul went to the foot of the stairs and shouted, "Luke! Come down here."

Luke came into the kitchen and stood with his head down. "Where's Agatha?" demanded Toni.

"I don't know," he said. "She left that note."

"I bet she didn't," said Simon. "Bet you wrote it yourself."

"That's enough!" said Paul. "Stop accusing my son of lying and get out of here."

"If I can't find her by this evening," said Toni, "I'm calling the police."

Out in the yard, Simon said, "What do we do now?"

"Start looking around. Look. There are two sets of footprints. One large, one small, heading out of the yard." They followed the muddy prints to the edge of a field and stood looking around.

"I don't think he would actually kill her," said Toni. "Maybe do something to give her a scare. Maybe lock her up somewhere, but it wouldn't be in any of the buildings near the farm, because she could shout and be heard."

"Let's follow the path round the edge of the fields," said Toni.

Farther on, they again found the footprints

in a muddy patch. "Keep going," urged Toni.

"Look at that," said Simon. A watery sunlight had broken through the clouds and was gilding the fields. "There's the roof of something away ahead."

They hurried on along the fields until they came to a dilapidated stone building. The door was fastened with a new padlock.

"Agatha!" called Toni.

A voice from somewhere above their heads said, "Up here!"

They both stood back and looked up at the roof. There was a hole in the slates and Agatha's head was poking through.

"Don't try to get out that way," called Toni. "The rest of the roof might be rotten. We'll try to break the door."

Simon found a loose stone and began to hammer at the padlock until Toni said, "The hinges are pretty rotten and rusty. Try them."

Simon hammered at the hinges until two of them on the left splintered. Together, they heaved open the door.

Agatha was gingerly climbing down from the top of two old cabin trunks balanced on two beer crates.

They rushed to help her down.

"Snakes and bastards!" howled Agatha.

"I'll kill that monster."

"Luke?" asked Toni, brushing cobwebs off Agatha's coat.

"That's him. How did you guess? Did he confess?"

"No, he left a note, supposed to come from you," said Simon, "saying you didn't want to go through with the marriage."

Agatha sat down suddenly on an upturned beer crate.

"Did you really want to be a farmer's wife?" asked Toni.

The rain came down again and some drops fell through the hole in the roof and a rising wind howled round the building.

"I made a mistake," said Agatha sadly. She slowly drew off her engagement ring.

"Should I call the police?" asked Toni.

"No, leave it," said Agatha. "I want to forget about the whole sorry thing."

Toni helped her to her feet and together, with heads bowed against the driving rain, they walked back to the farmhouse.

"Blast! He's hidden my car," said Agatha. "It can't be far. I've got the keys. Try round the side of the house or the barn or something."

Simon finally called from the barn. "It's round the side here covered in bales of hay."

Then Agatha marched into the farmhouse

where Paul was sitting at the kitchen table going over some accounts.

She put the ring on the table and told him in a weary voice what had happened.

"He's gone out," said Paul. "Are you going to charge him?"

"No, I'm sick of the whole thing," said Agatha. "He's hidden my car by the barn. Go and help Simon get it out."

Paul got to his feet, looking sad and defeated. "Has this happened before?" asked Agatha.

"Once," he said miserably. "Luke blames me for the breakup of our marriage."

"I never asked you," said Agatha, "what happened to your marriage?"

"She said she found the work too hard."

"Work!" Agatha's rosy dreams of being a sort of Marie Antoinette and playing at farming suddenly seemed stupid. She had assumed Paul would have plenty of help inside and outside the farmhouse.

"Why didn't you hire help for her?" she asked.

"The farm was going through a bad patch. I just couldn't afford the help."

"So was my money the attraction?"

"No, no. Darling, don't say that."

"It's over," said Agatha. "Get my car and let me get out of here!"

■ . ■ ■

When Agatha curled up in bed that night, she found to her surprise that she was not grieving or upset. When love got a blow, it was heart-wrenching, but when sex left, nothing remained but rather distasteful memories as if she had eaten too many chocolates.

Something was tugging at the back of her mind about the Winter Parva murders, but she was too tired to stay awake to try to figure out what it was.

On the following Saturday, she paid a visit to Mrs. Bloxby to tell her what had happened.

"I think you mixed up rich landowner with farmer," said Mrs. Bloxby. "After a divorce, it is difficult for the children. We once had an unpleasant incident at a wedding. A woman was marrying again, and they were having the old-fashioned wedding service. It got to the bit about anyone objecting to the marriage or forever holding their peace, when the daughter, one of the bridesmaids, started shouting her mother was a whore. She read out the names of five men she claimed her mother had enjoyed affairs with. The bridegroom just turned round and fled out of the church."

"And was it true? About the lovers, I mean?" asked Agatha.

"It seems to have been, and the bride was all in virginal white, too."

"I didn't think your husband would want to marry her anyway."

"He didn't know, you see," said Mrs. Bloxby. "She had only recently moved into the village. Are you very upset about the end of your engagement?"

"No, but I do feel a bit sorry for Paul although I am sure my money was some of the attraction. I should never have agreed to marry him."

"Have you seen Charles?" asked Mrs. Bloxby. "I saw the announcement of his engagement."

"Haven't seen him at all or heard from him," said Agatha.

Later that afternoon, Bill Wong called on her. Agatha made him coffee and asked him for the latest news.

"There isn't any," said Bill. "Jed has been remanded in custody, still claiming to be responsible for all the murders. Mrs. Crosswith is off the hook. I feel bad about it. Wilkes pressured him into the confession.

But there's no proof. That's what worries me. I'm sure a murderer is still out there. I still suspect John Hale. He needs money. He could have bumped off Bert Simple, George Southern could have known about it and so got murdered as well. Now Hale is free to marry the widow."

"I've lost touch," said Agatha. "When's the wedding?"

"Next month."

"I might just pay him a call."

"Now, that's silly. If you suspect him of being a murderer and confront him, you may be next."

"I'll call on him at the school."

"And he may do nothing there, but try to catch you later. Don't."

"Just an idea," said Agatha.

"So you're getting married," said Bill, changing the subject.

"Not anymore. I made a mistake. What about you?"

"Nothing yet," said Bill. "I live in hope."

Agatha found herself restless that evening. The whole business of the Winter Parva murders nagged at her mind. She looked up the local paper. There was a performance of *The Pirates of Penzance* on at the Mircester theatre. Should she go there? Why not?

Maybe she could catch him before the show. She fished in the blue bag supplied by the council for cardboard and took out an old FedEx envelope and sealed it up again. She changed into a black sweater and trousers and pulled a baseball cap down over her eyes, hoping that she looked like a FedEx messenger.

At the stage door, Agatha said to the stage doorkeeper, "Special delivery for John Hale."

"Hand it over," he said.

"Got to sign for it personally," said Agatha.

"Oh, go on up. Door with the star on."

Agatha hurried up the stairs until she found the right door and walked straight in. John Hale, wearing a pirate's costume, was seated in front of a mirror. He glared at Agatha's reflection and said, "What do you want?"

"I want to know why you are marrying Gwen."

"Get out! That's none of your business."

"It is, in a way," said Agatha. "If you are in love with Gwen, what were you doing romancing me?"

"Look at yourself in the mirror, *dear.* Money, that's what."

"And so that is the attraction of Gwen?"

"No, I've always loved her. I never thought I would have a chance, and then I found out she loved me. So, shove off."

"Did you kill Bert Simple?"

He picked up a pot of cleansing cream and hurled it at her. Agatha ducked and then beat a hasty retreat.

Well, that didn't really get me anywhere, thought Agatha as she turned into the lane leading to her cottage. In her headlamps, she saw to her dismay that Paul and Luke were standing on her doorstep. She was about to make a U-turn but Paul saw her and waved. Agatha drove up slowly, parked and got out of the car.

"What is it?" she asked.

"Luke wants to apologise to you. Go on, Luke."

"I'm ever so sorry," he said. "Dad's all cut up and he really loves you. Forgive me?"

"Oh, all right," said Agatha grumpily. "Now, if you'll both stand aside, I'd —"

"Oh, do talk to me, Agatha," pleaded Paul. "Run along, Luke."

Luke got on a motorbike and roared off. "Come in for a drink, Paul," said Agatha. "But I can't change my mind."

Once they were seated in Agatha's living room, Paul said quietly, "Did our night together mean nothing to you, Agatha?"

Agatha cringed inside. But she said, "Let's forget about it. I made a mistake."

"I don't go in for one-night stands," said Paul, "and Luke is really sorry."

"I don't go in for one-night stands either," said Agatha. "I really thought it would work out. But I am afraid we don't have much in common. I want to go on being a detective, married or not, and that wouldn't be much use to you in a wife."

"I've a damn good mind to sue you for breach of promise," said Paul, becoming angry.

"And part of my defence could well be the attack on me by your son," said Agatha.

Paul stood up and glared down at her. "You are a bitch!"

"Think what a lucky escape you've had," said Agatha.

He stomped out and then to her relief, she heard the front door slam.

Agatha felt miserable and grubby. After all, she had led him on and she had gone to bed with him. She felt like crying. But she roused herself to make a sandwich for supper. She didn't feel like cooking a meal.

She tossed and turned in bed and then fell into deep sleep. Agatha awoke with the sound of her cats mewing and jumping on her bed.

She struggled up. "What's up?" she asked. Her cats looked frantic. And then she smelled petrol. She pulled on her dressing down and ran downstairs. Someone was pouring petrol through the letterbox.

Agatha ran into the kitchen and seized a large fire extinguisher. She covered the small tide of petrol with foam and yelled, "I've called the police!"

A lighted wad of cotton was shoved through the letterbox. But the flames fizzled out in the carpet of foam.

Trembling all over but frightened to open the door, she called the police, having only pretended to before. Her legs seemed to have turned to jelly. She sat down on the kitchen floor and hugged her knees while her cats circled around her.

At last, she heard the blessed sound of a siren.

First there were the uniformed police and then shortly afterwards Bill Wong and Alice arrived.

"Any idea who's behind this?" asked Bill.

Agatha had already been asked this question by the uniformed police and had said she did not know. But now she said, "I went to see John Hale at the theatre."

"I told you not to," said Bill. "So what happened?"

Agatha told him about her visit.

"We'll check up on his movements. Any other suspect? See anyone else this evening?"

"No," lied Agatha. She felt she had hurt Paul enough without throwing suspicion on Luke. She could only hope no one in the village had seen them. James Lacey's cottage was next to hers but he was not at home.

The questioning went on while a forensic team checked outside.

When they had all finally left, Agatha went up to her bedroom, got dressed and packed a suitcase. She put her cats in their cat boxes and loaded them in her car along with her suitcase. She left the cats with her cleaner, Doris Simpson, after waking her to tell her what had happened.

Then she drove to the George Hotel in Mircester and checked herself into a room. In the morning, she phoned Paul and asked him if Luke had been with him all night.

"Of course," he said stiffly. "Why?"

Agatha told him of the attempt to burn down her cottage.

"My son is a good boy," said Paul. "If you send the police round here, I'll never forgive you."

"You'll never forgive me anyway," said Agatha sadly and hung up.

CHAPTER EIGHT

Two days later, Agatha was summoned to police headquarters. In an interrogation room, she was faced by Bill Wong and Alice Peterson.

"Mrs. Raisin," began Bill formally, "do you know Luke Newton?"

"Yes, he's the son of a man I was briefly dating. Why?"

"His fingerprints were on your door. The tyre marks on the wet muddy road outside your cottage match the tyres on his motor-bike."

"I forgot to tell you," said Agatha desperately, "that he and his father called on me earlier in the evening, so that probably explains it."

"And what was the reason for the visit?"

"Oh, just social," said Agatha airily.

"You were engaged to Paul Newton, but broke off the engagement, is that correct?"

"Well, yes."

"So why did they call on you?"

Agatha's mind worked rapidly. If she told them about Luke's apology, Bill would want to know what he was apologising for. He could go to court. His defence could well be that he was furious with her for breaking his father's heart and that one-night stand would be brought out.

"It was a social call. We parted on good terms."

Bill studied a sheet of paper. What had Paul said? wondered Agatha.

"Yes, Mr. Newton says he joined you in your cottage for a drink and his son went off to join his friends in Mircester. I don't believe either him or you.

"Don't you wonder why we have Luke Newton's fingerprints? Two years ago, his father became engaged to a widow. Her name is Bertha Summerhayes. Luke sent her letters, threatening to kill her if she married his father. He finally met her in the street and punched her hard. He was arrested and brought to court. As it was a first offence, he was only given community service. So what are you not telling me?"

"Nothing," said Agatha, studying the table in front of her. "What about John Hale?"

"Mr. Hale went to a party in Mircester after the show. It went on until three in the morning. There is no way he could have travelled to Carsely. So let's get back to Paul Newton and his son."

"You'd never have thought Bill was a friend of mine," confided Agatha to Mrs. Bloxby that evening. "He just hammered on and on with the questions."

"Don't you feel it might have been wiser to tell him the truth?" said Mrs. Bloxby.

"And have me slated in court as a heartless man-eating harridan?"

"Better than being dead."

"Oh, it won't come to that. I phoned Paul and told him how I rescued his precious son from prison."

"Did he believe you?"

"Well . . . not exactly."

Mrs. Bloxby hesitated and then said gently, "Is it really so important to get married to . . . just, well, *anyone*?"

"I like the idea of having a man around the place," said Agatha, "and not some sort of fly-by-night like Charles."

"Perhaps Sir Charles is a good idea. You have occasional male company and yet you keep your independence."

"But he's getting married and he never even bothered to tell me," complained Agatha.

"Did you tell him about your engagement?"

"No. But I was angry with him about not telling me about his."

"Of course, he may not go through with it," said the vicar's wife.

Agatha wondered at her own sudden surge of hope. "What makes you say that?"

"He has been engaged in the past and it has never worked out."

When Agatha returned to her cottage, it was to find Charles sitting on her kitchen floor playing with her cats.

"What's been going on?" he asked, smiling up at her. "I phoned your office but I was told you were being grilled at the police station because someone tried to set your cottage alight."

"Oh, that." Agatha took off her coat and slung it over the back of a kitchen chair. "My engagement's off. It was my ex-fiancé's son. Didn't want me to marry Dad and that was after I had decided I didn't want to marry him either. What about you?"

He grinned. "That's why I'm here. Got an invitation for you to the wedding."

"Thanks," said Agatha bleakly. "When is it?"

"July tenth."

"I might be abroad."

"Try not to be."

"Are you happy?" asked Agatha.

"As usual. Why?"

"Well, deeply in love."

"You've been reading those romances again. She's very suitable."

"Rich?"

"Very."

Agatha sighed. "You *are* mercenary, Charles."

"I've got to be. That estate of mine drinks money. And I've got the threat that the government might bring in that mansion tax. As if I weren't paying lots in tax already." He got to his feet. "Feel like some dinner?"

"No thanks. I want an early night."

When he had left, Agatha began to feel nervous. She had only spent one night at the hotel but felt sorely tempted to pack up again and seek refuge at the George.

"Don't be a wimp," she said out loud. She suddenly wished she had accepted Charles's invitation to dinner. But somehow, she felt hurt that he was abandoning her. Had their time together meant nothing to him?

Two days later, as Agatha drove to work, she saw in amazement that the sun was shining down from a cloudless sky. The long-awaited spring seemed to have arrived at last.

She felt a lifting of her heart and remembered Mrs. Bloxby's words. What on earth had she been thinking of to want to rush into marriage with a man she didn't even love? She had a warm feeling of being restored to sanity after a period of madness. She blamed the recent awful weather and the horrors of the Winter Parva murders. For once in her life, vowed Agatha, she would let the police do their job.

In the office, she cheerfully set about allocating cases for the day. She was just about to go out on another divorce case when a nervous-looking woman came into the office.

"You've got to help me," she cried. "The police aren't doing anything."

Agatha urged her to sit down and tell her what it was all about. "What is your name?" asked Agatha.

"Rose Alexander," she said. "My daughter, Kylie, didn't come home last night. Her friends say she was about to get on the bus after school but then she said she had left something in the classroom and would find her own way home."

"How old is Kylie?" asked Agatha.

"She's fifteen. What can have happened to her?"

"Where is your home?"

"Winter Parva. You see what I mean? All those murders and Kylie disappeared."

"Has she gone missing before?"

"Never. Oh, she's been late a couple of times but she always came home."

"When she was late home, where had she been?"

"She said she'd been with her friend, Maisie Green, just hanging about."

"Give me your address and Maisie's address," said Agatha. "Have you a photograph?"

Mrs. Alexander took a photo out of her handbag. It showed a surly-looking girl with a fat face and a nose stud.

"I'll start on it right away," said Agatha.

"I don't have that much money. But I'm desperate."

"Let's see if I can do anything," said Agatha. "I won't charge you much."

When Mrs. Alexander had left, Agatha asked Toni and Simon where two young girls might hang out, adding, "Must be Mircester. There's nothing in that cursed village."

"There's a disco called Nice Nights,

round the back of the market square," said Simon. "But they don't open up until seven in the evening."

"I'll see if there's anyone there," said Agatha.

Agatha hammered on the door of the disco until an unshaven young man opened it. She introduced herself and said she wanted information on a missing teenager.

"I'm the barman," he said. "I've been checking the stocks. I don't think I can help you. There are so many of them in the evening."

"Just have a look at this photo," said Agatha, holding it out to him.

"Oh, her. Yes, she got stroppy when I wouldn't serve her any drink."

"How did you know she was underage? They all look so mature these days."

"Get this. The little tart was in her school uniform. Then a man came up and bought a drink and I saw him taking it to her so I got the bouncer and got them both thrown out."

"Do you know who the man was?"

"Sure. A regular. Tim Eliot. Plumber."

"Where does he live?"

"Dunno."

■ ■ ■ ■

Agatha retreated to her car and looked up phone numbers and addresses in the Mircester phone book she kept in her car.

There was a T. Eliot listed. The address was in one of the tower blocks on the edge of the town.

She drove there and found the lift wasn't working. Glad he only lived on the fourth floor, Agatha made her way up the filthy stairs. Considering the amount plumbers charge, she thought, you'd think he'd have found a better place to live.

Agatha stood outside his door, put her ear to the door and listened.

She heard a girl's voice say, "I'd better get home or Ma will have the filth looking for me."

"Aw, quit moaning and come back to bed," said a man's voice.

Agatha retreated, thinking that she had no real muscle in her agency and she did not feel like tackling the plumber alone.

She retreated down the stairs and phoned the police and then stood and waited until a police car arrived.

Agatha told the police about the missing girl and waited until they went up the stairs.

She was still wearing her winter clothes. The sun was hot. She took off her coat and left it in the car.

After a time, a girl Agatha recognised from the photo was escorted by the police along with a small, slight man who Agatha judged to be in his late thirties.

Kylie looked mulish and insolent. Poor Mrs. Alexander, thought Agatha. I won't charge her anything. She's got enough on her plate.

She phoned Mrs. Alexander and told her what had happened and told her she would pick her up and take her to police headquarters.

As she drove the distressed mother back to Mircester, she told her gently that Eliot would likely be charged with having sex with a minor. Mrs. Alexander began to cry, and cried all the way back to Mircester. Agatha left her at police headquarters and with a sigh, decided to get to work on that divorce case. She phoned Phil and told him to meet her. Best to be armed with a photographer.

She arrived back at the office, later that afternoon, tired and frustrated, for so far she had not found the necessary proof of infidelity, to find Mrs. Alexander waiting for her.

"I'm ever so grateful to you," said Mrs. Alexander. "My poor Kylie says she's awfully sorry and it'll never happen again."

Until the next time, thought Agatha.

She saw Mrs. Alexander was opening her battered handbag to reveal crumpled bank notes.

"There's no fee," said Agatha hurriedly. "The police did all the work."

"But it was you that found my girl!"

"Never mind. Put your money away. Would you like a coffee?"

"Yes, please."

Agatha went over to the coffee machine in the corner. "What does your husband think of all this?" she asked.

"He ran away after Kylie was born."

"Oh, dear. Milk and sugar?"

"Just black."

Agatha handed her a mug of coffee. "It's so good of you," said Mrs. Alexander. "You must be working overtime on those murders in our village. Mind you, the way Bert Simple went on, it's no surprise he was murdered."

"In what way?"

"He beat his poor wife."

"What! The saintly Gwen. Why did no one tell me about this?"

"I think everyone felt it was bad to speak ill of the dead. But Gwen'll be all right now. She can marry Mr. Hale and Walt can go to the uni like he always wanted to."

"Did Bert stop him going?"

"That he did. He wanted Walt and his missus to go on slaving in that bakery. They're selling it now."

After she had left, Agatha sat down at her computer and began to go through all her notes on the Winter Parva murders. A motive at last! And surely a strong one.

The fact that this seemed to be the one case she had never solved began to infuriate her. Without stopping to consider that she might be putting herself in danger, she set off for Winter Parva.

CHAPTER NINE

The sun was setting as Agatha drove into Winter Parva and parked in front of the bakery. The air at the end of the street had the soft bluish tinge of an early-spring evening. Blackbirds were singing from the rooftops.

The bakery was closed but Agatha could see there were still lights on in the shop. She knocked at the door.

It was opened by Walt Simple. He was a handsome boy, thought Agatha, who had never looked at him closely before. He had thick fair hair and a square face and firm mouth.

"I thought you were selling the bakery," said Agatha. "I don't see any sign."

"Private deal," he said. "Henley's Wines are buying it."

"So the villagers are losing their only bakery?"

"Screw the villagers," he said rudely.

"What do you want?"

"I wanted a quick word with you and your mother," said Agatha.

He eyed her narrowly and then jerked his head in the direction of the back shop. Agatha walked past him and he slammed the door behind her.

He then moved in front of her and raised the flap on the counter so that she could pass through. Agatha suddenly began to wish she had not come and had communicated her suspicions to Bill Wong instead.

Gwen was seated in her little parlour watching an Australian soap on television. When she saw Agatha, she reluctantly switched it off and asked, "What do you want?"

"I came to congratulate you on your forthcoming marriage," said Agatha weakly.

Gwen looked her up and down slowly. "And?"

"And," said Agatha, "something's come up."

"Sit down."

Agatha sat down at the table. Gwen sat facing her. Walt sat beside his mother and took her hand.

"I have just received news that your late husband beat you and was preventing your son from going to university," said Agatha, deciding to plunge in.

"Who on earth told you that load of lies?" demanded Walt.

"Just a contact."

"My husband was a good man," said Gwen. "Who are you to sully his memory? Walt, get her out of here."

Walt stood up. He walked round the table and jerked Agatha roughly to her feet and frog-marched her out of the shop.

As the bakery door slammed behind her, Agatha stood irresolute. Surely other people in the village must know if what Mrs. Alexander had told her was true.

Then she remembered the village gossip, Marie Tench, who lived in a flat above the newspaper shop.

To her relief, Marie Tench was at home and peered at her curiously over the massive barrier of her hitched-up bosoms.

Agatha refused an offer of tea or coffee and said, "I have just learned that Bert Simple was a wife beater. Know anything about that?"

"How much?"

"How much what?" demanded Agatha.

"I want a hundred pounds."

"Fifty," said Agatha.

"Oh, all right. Fork it out."

Agatha took a ten and two twenties out of her wallet and passed them over. "I hope what you've got to tell me is worth it," she said, "or I'll take that money back."

Marie stuffed the money down into her capacious brassiere. "Well, it's like this. About a month before Bert got killed, I was in the shop. I was the only customer. Walt wasn't behind the counter but there was one hell of a row going on in the back shop. Gwen was sobbing and Walt was shouting, 'Leave my mother alone.' Then there was a crash and I could hear Gwen crying. There was a long silence and I wondered whether to leave but they do cream meringues and I wanted some so I called, 'Shop!' Nothing happened and I was about to turn away, when Walt came out. He had a cut lip.

"I asked what was going on and he said they had found a rat in the back shop and had been chasing it to kill it."

"Were the police ever called to the bakery?" asked Agatha.

"Not that I heard."

"Why didn't you talk about this before?"

"Because it couldn't have anything to do with the murder. Gwen and her son were in the theatre that night."

"But the trap was probably rigged before the performance," said Agatha. "Didn't anyone think of that?"

"Well, the police were asking everyone for alibis. If there had been anything fishy about Gwen and Walt's alibis, they'd have taken them in. It wasn't any of the villagers' place to tell the police anything. Gwen's happy now and we need the bakery."

"You won't have it for much longer," said Agatha. "It's been sold to a wine company."

"They can't do that!"

"They have."

"Where am I supposed to go for my cakes now?" wailed Marie. "The supermarkets sell doughy rubbish."

"When is Gwen's wedding?"

"Next week, on Wednesday at two in the afternoon."

When Agatha left she was torn between a desire to tell Bill Wong what she had found out and a longing to close the case herself. But she realised that Bill could not really do anything. Gwen and her son must have good alibis. Wilkes was sure he had the murderer. All at once, she missed the support of Charles. But Charles was to be married as well.

She decided to wait and attend the wedding, where she could study Walt and Gwen closely.

■ ■ ■ ■

Caroline Featherington, Charles's fiancée, was having dinner that evening with Jessica Barnard, an old school friend. After they had reminisced about their school days, Jessica cast a jealous look at the sparkling engagement ring on Caroline's finger.

"I hope your Charles has given up seeing that detective woman," she said.

"What detective woman?"

"That female, Agatha Raisin. Runs a detective agency in Mircester."

"And what on earth has that to do with Charles?"

"Do you remember Buffy Norton?"

"Vaguely," said Caroline.

"Well, Buffy was in St. Tropez last year and your Charles and this Raisin woman were all lovey-dovey on holiday together."

"He must be mistaken," said Caroline in a firm voice. "Let's talk about something else."

After dinner, Caroline drove straight to Charles's mansion. She found him in the library, with his feet up, reading a book.

"I want you to tell me and tell me *now,* what is your relationship with a woman called Agatha Raisin?"

"We're friends. Don't glare at me."

"What were you doing holidaying with her in the south of France?"

"Oh, that."

"Yes that."

"The old girl was pretty shattered after a nasty murder case. I took her on holiday."

"She's old?"

"Sorry for her," said Charles. "Too old for detective work. Come here and give me a kiss."

But Caroline could not shake off her doubts. Her parents had only reluctantly agreed to the wedding, saying that Charles had a reputation for being mean and had once been heard to declare he would only marry for money.

She sat at her computer and looked up Agatha on the Internet. Agatha looked well dressed and attractive in a pugnacious sort of way.

Caroline began to worry. She was not in love with Charles but she was shortly about to reach her thirtieth birthday and she did want to get married. She could not imagine why no one had proposed to her before. She was a very tall girl with lank hair and a domineering manner. But she had an amazing ego and when she looked in her mirror, all she saw was a graceful and attractive woman.

She then googled the agency's Web site and studied the list of cases they usually covered. Caroline decided that she would claim to have lost a pet dog and that way she could meet Agatha and study the woman for herself.

Caroline was unfortunate in that Agatha had recently visited the dentist to get her teeth cleaned, and, in an old copy of *Cotswold Life,* she had found a photograph of Caroline at a hunt ball with Charles.

So the next morning when she arrived at the agency, Agatha recognised her. She gave a fictitious name and handed over a photograph of the dog she said was missing. It was actually a photograph of her dog Brutus, who had died two years before.

Agatha took down details of the dog that was supposed to have been lost and when. Her suspicions that Caroline had come to look her over were confirmed when Caroline said, "Do you know a friend of mine, Charles Fraith?"

Now Agatha would dearly have loved an opportunity to sabotage Charles's engagement, but her better nature took over and she said, "Yes, I haven't seen him in ages.

Give him my regards."

Caroline was partly reassured, except that the photograph on the Internet had not done Agatha justice. She had glossy brown hair, a fairly good figure, long legs and she was impeccably dressed.

Agatha was just beginning to say, "Mrs. Freedman will give you a contract to sign and then I will ask you some more questions," when the door crashed open and Paul Newton strode in. "Give me one more chance, Agatha," he pleaded. "Luke is so very sorry and won't interfere again."

"I'm sorry, Paul," said Agatha. "It's really all over."

Caroline stared, alarmed. Paul was handsome and yet this wretched woman was not interested!

"I've changed my mind," Caroline said suddenly. She followed the rejected Paul down the stairs and caught up with him in the street outside.

"I need your advice," she said. "Can we go somewhere for a coffee?"

Paul was as tall as she was. He listened to the cut-glass voice and quickly assessed the price of what she was wearing.

"Yes, all right," he said. "We'll go to the coffee room in the George. It'll be quiet this early in the day."

■ ■ ■ ■

Seated over coffee and croissants in the comforting gloom of the old coffee room, Caroline poured out her troubles. Paul's face darkened. "I should have known she was a heartless flirt," he raged.

"But I don't know if Charles is still interested in her," wailed Caroline.

"I know, let's play detective and investigate the detective," said Paul. "But I should not think an attractive lady like yourself has anything to worry about."

Caroline brightened. "What do you do?"

"I'm a farmer."

"We have three tenant farms on our estate. I say, Charles is busy today. Would you like to see them?"

Paul agreed, his mind thinking, tenant farms, must be really loaded.

They spent a happy morning. Caroline knew a lot about farming and they discussed crops and livestock. He was invited to lunch and met her parents, Colonel and Mrs. Featherington.

After he had left, Caroline's father said, "Now there's a real man. Not like that flighty chap, Charles Fraith."

■ ■ ■ ■

Charles was bored and he realised Agatha never bored him and he missed her company. So when Agatha arrived home, it was to find him in her living room, happily watching television, with her cats on his lap.

"What are you doing here?" snapped Agatha. "I had a visit from your fiancée this morning, using an assumed name and asking me if I knew you."

"And what did you say?"

"I said yes and I hadn't seen you in months."

"Well, that's all right," he said lazily.

"To add to the fun," said Agatha, sinking down wearily beside him on the sofa, "my ex-fiancé crashed in begging me to reconsider. Your Caroline said she'd changed her mind about employing me to find a lost dog and left as well."

"What an exciting life you do lead," said Charles, "and how boring mine is of late. Got any farther with the Winter Parva murders?"

Agatha helped herself to a gin and tonic and sat down beside him again and began to talk about all the latest developments.

■ ■ ■ ■

Outside, seated in Caroline's car — the latest Audi, Paul noticed appreciatively — they waited and watched. "Are you sure that's Charles's car?" asked Paul.

"Yes, of course I'm sure. If she's just a friend and he leaves to go home, then it's all right. But if he stays the night, the engagement is definitely off."

"Get down! The door's opening."

Agatha and Charles came out and got into Agatha's car. "Let's follow them," said Paul.

They drove to a Thai restaurant in Evesham and took a table at the window. Charles looked across the street and recognised Caroline's car parked opposite. He hated being spied on. He was hungry and he was determined to enjoy his meal.

Agatha was saying, "I might go to Winter Parva tomorrow and see if I can pick up any more gossip."

"I'll come with you," said Charles, thinking, I may as well give dear Caroline something to really worry about. "Did you really not want to get married, Agatha?"

"It did seem tempting until his son tried to kill me twice."

"Tell me about it."

So Agatha did. She had nearly finished her tale when she looked at him wide-eyed and clutched his hand.

"Gwen's son!" she exclaimed.

"What about him?"

"Say he's like Luke. Say he's close to his mother and hates his father. So he bumps off his father. George Southern has something on him so he bumps George off as well."

"But Gwen is getting married again, isn't she? So if he were that possessive, he'd kill John."

"Blast! There is one missing bit. Kimberley Buxton. She claimed she was assaulted by Bert Simple and yet it was all hushed up. Her father got the blacksmith to sharpen that sword."

"We'll go tomorrow," said Charles.

"Hadn't you better phone your fiancée?"

Charles glanced out the window. He was furious with Caroline for spying on him.

"No, I won't bother," he said.

Back in Carsely, Caroline and Paul waited for Charles to leave Agatha's cottage but the time dragged on until they saw all the lights in the cottage going out.

"That's it," said Caroline bitterly. "I don't

want to speak to him again. I'll take you back to my place and you can pick up your car."

As she drove back up out of the village, Paul said tentatively, "This may be the wrong time to ask, but what about us seeing more of each other? I do enjoy your company."

"I'd like that," said Caroline slowly. "I'd like that a lot."

As Charles and Agatha drove off the following morning, Charles was very quiet. He was wondering at his own folly of having spent the night in Agatha's cottage. He was sure the spying Caroline would have followed them back to Carsely. He wondered whether he should phone her and explain things, but he had been so bored since his engagement, despite the fact that he had kept telling himself he was doing the right thing.

He would leave it to her, he thought lazily. If she really cared for him, she would demand an explanation and he would deal with it then.

Spring had finally arrived in the Cotswolds. The trees shimmered in the sunlight with bright new green leaves and daffodils raised their golden trumpets to the sky as if in celebration.

David Buxton was not at home and Kimberley was at school, but Mrs. Buxton answered the door to them. She looked frightened and alarmed when they asked if Bert Simple had really attempted to sexually molest Kimberley.

"It was all a bad joke," she said, her thin arms hugged across her flat chest. "Go away. Why can't you leave it alone?"

She slammed the door in their faces.

"Frightened to death," said Agatha.

"Where next?" asked Charles.

"Maybe we should try Bessie Burdock. She was in that pantomime. I'd like to know more about Gwen's marriage."

Bessie Burdock drove the screaming toddlers she was looking after into the garden and settled down for a chat.

In answer to their questions, she said, "I don't know if Bert beat her and that's a fact. There was a bit of talk. But Gwen always looked so cool and elegant. There was one thing, I bring to mind, now that you ask. It was about three years ago, Gwen and her son Walt were at a village dance. Gwen looked lovely. She was dancing with her son and I swear they looked like a couple. Gwen never showed her years. Bert bursts into the dance and orders both of them home. Walt said they were staying and his father punched him in the face. Someone started shouting about calling the police and Bert got all oily like and said he'd been drinking and he was sorry and then he just left.

"Walt and Gwen sat together for a bit, talking quietly and then they left, too."

"So," said Agatha outside. "There's a big motive."

"But Gwen is getting married and happy ever after and all that," said Charles.

"I'm going to that wedding next week," said Agatha. "I want to see if the couple are really happy and if Walt is happy as well."

When Charles got home, his man, Gustav, handed him a small package. "This was shoved through the letterbox," he said.

Charles took the package into his study and opened it. It contained a small jewellery box with the ring he had given Caroline inside. There was no note.

He sat down slowly. He should really phone and ask for an explanation, but all his life he had avoided confrontations as much as possible, so he lazily decided just to wait and see what happened.

He would attend that wedding with Agatha. Like her, he was curious to see the happy pair.

The day of the wedding dawned bright and sunny. It was unseasonably warm. People shook their heads and said that this was the only summer they were likely to get, for when the real British summer came around, it would probably be as wet as usual.

Charles was dressed casually and Agatha, thinking that as she was not an official guest and there was no need to wear a hat, was wearing a cool dark blue silk trouser suit.

After Caroline, thought Charles, Agatha's company was like slipping into a comfortable pair of slippers after wearing shoes that pinched.

Guessing that John Hale's side of the church would not have many people while Gwen's would be crowded with the villagers, Agatha said to the usher, "Friends of the groom."

Mrs. Bloxby's husband was to perform the wedding ceremony. Agatha and Charles were seated in a pew at the back of the church. At one point, Agatha stood up and looked around, hoping to see Mrs. Bloxby, but she was nowhere in sight.

The sun shone down through the old stained glass windows. The church was fragrant with the scent of flowers and incense. The organ played softly. The crowd whispered in anticipation as Walt took his place at the front of the church.

"But where's John?" muttered Agatha.

The organist broke into the opening strains of the wedding march. Agatha twisted her head and looked round at the church porch. Gwen stood there flanked by two bridesmaids. She was wearing a mediaeval dress of gold silk embroidered with seed pearls. On her head was a small Juliet cap and her long hair was worn loose.

Walt turned and saw his mother and hurried down the aisle. Agatha could hear frantic whispering.

Agatha got up, followed by Charles. Gwen was retreating to her wedding limousine.

The two bridesmaids were standing outside. "What's going on?" asked Agatha, approaching them.

"John's late," said one.

Agatha and Charles returned to the church to sit down and wait and see if John turned up.

After half an hour, Walt strode up to the altar and addressed the company.

"I don't know what's happened to John. Please go along to the reception in the village hall."

"I don't like this one bit," said Agatha. "I keep thinking how Paul's son tried to kill me."

"Agatha, let's go to the police. Normally, they wouldn't investigate. But maybe you could convince them to go to his flat and break the door down."

Wilkes appeared cynical but said he would send Bill Wong round to have a look. Agatha and Charles drove after Bill's car to John's address. When they began to follow him up the stairs, Bill turned round and said, "Wait outside. This is police business."

"You wouldn't be here if it weren't for us," said Agatha stubbornly.

Bill knocked loudly at the door. There was no reply.

"Break the door down!" urged Agatha.

"I can't do that," protested Bill. "I need a warrant."

Charles stepped in front of Bill and tried the door handle. The door was unlocked. Bill went in, calling, "Mr. Hale!"

The living room and bedroom in the small apartment were empty. On the table by the window was a typed note. Bill fished out a pair of latex gloves and picked it up. He read: "Dear Gwen and Walt, I am so sorry, I can't go through with it. I am going abroad. All my love, John."

"It's not signed," said Bill.

"So anyone could have typed that," said Agatha.

Walt burst into the flat. "Where is the bastard?" he shouted. "Mum is crying her eyes out."

"He has left a note to the effect that he can't go through with it. No, don't touch the note. When did you last see him?"

"Last night," said Walt. "We had a stag party for him in the green room at the theatre."

"Play any tricks on him?" asked Bill.

"No. I can't understand it," said Walt. "He seemed happy."

"Why would he go and leave the door unlocked?" asked Agatha.

"Everyone out," ordered Bill. "I'll send a forensic team round."

Charles took himself off. Agatha went to her office and asked Patrick Mulligan to get in touch with his police contacts and find out if the forensic team had discovered anything sinister. Agatha did not believe that the note was genuine.

Patrick phoned her that evening to say that there were signs that John had really left. His toothbrush and shaving kit were gone along with clothes and his passport. No signs so far of any violence.

When Agatha rang off, she wondered whether Walt were like Luke. Perhaps he didn't want his mother to marry. Maybe he had killed John. Well, let's imagine, thought Agatha, that he killed John but somewhere outside the theatre. Where would he hide a body?

In the morning, she held a conference with her staff, asking them if they had any suggestions.

"I'd dump it in that pond," said Simon. "Say Walt did murder John, then he would assume the police would never look there, that is, if by the remote chance they thought John had been murdered. I've got scuba diving equipment. I'll go down there this evening if you like and take a look around."

"Good idea," said Agatha. "One of us had better come with you as a lookout."

"What about Toni?" asked Simon.

"I've got a date," lied Toni.

"I'll go," volunteered Patrick.

"Good," said Agatha. "I'm going back to Winter Parva to see if anyone will gossip to me now. I'll start with Pixie Turner."

To Agatha's surprise, Pixie Turner welcomed her instead of trying to get rid of her as she had done before. Now that there was no possibility of any press arriving, Pixie was devoid of make-up and wearing a faded T-shirt and jeans.

"Isn't it awful John disappearing like that," said Pixie when she and Agatha were seated in the cluttered living room. "Poor Gwen. She must be devastated."

"Was Bert Simple a wife beater?" asked Agatha.

"I did hear a bit of gossip about that, but, look here, there's so much wife beating goes on in the Cotswolds, they should show it at some country fair as a rural pastime." She threw back her head and laughed, revealing squiggly discoloured teeth.

"Is Walt very close to his mother?"

"I guess so. Boys always are." Her eyes narrowed. "Hey, what are you getting at? Do you think Walt bumped off John because he's got one of those eedpussy something complexes?"

"No, and don't tell anyone anything about my questions."

"Wouldn't breathe a word. It's a shame the bakery's to be closed. The steak pie they served at the reception was ever so good. Isn't that interesting that you think Walt killed John."

"I never said that!" howled Agatha. "I don't want Walt Simple to sue me."

Simon appeared in the office at the end of the day. "Nothing in that awful pond but rubbish," he said.

"I wonder if there's anything going on in that village hall at the moment," said Agatha. "A body could be stuffed somewhere under that stage and no one would be the wiser. I'm going over there."

"I'd better come with you," said Toni.

"Are you sure?" asked Agatha. "I must admit I'd be glad of the company."

"I'll come too," said Simon quickly.

"No, it's all right. You're tired," said Agatha. "We'll have a bite to eat first, Toni. I'll feel more comfortable detecting after dark in that poxy village."

They went in Toni's old Ford, Agatha not wanting her own car to be recognised. They parked round the back of the village hall and got out. It was a soft spring evening. The stars above were just beginning to come out. It was the sort of evening when that perpetual teenager that lurked somewhere inside Agatha thought again about romance and the lack of it. Would her heart ever beat quickly again at the sight of some man? Falling in love was a heady drug and Agatha missed it.

They approached the side of the hall until they were in its black shadow. Toni took out a pencil torch. "That's the door there," whispered Agatha. "See if it's locked."

Toni tried the handle. "It's locked but I think I can spring it." She took a thin strip of metal out of a bag at her waist and slid it into the door and jerked. There was a click and the door sprang open.

Agatha took out her own torch. "I don't think we can risk switching on the lights."

They prowled around in the darkness. There were trunks full of costumes but not one contained a body, nor was there anything sinister behind old bits of scenery.

"Bad idea," said Agatha.

"Shh!" hissed Toni. "Someone's come onto the stage."

"Why on earth did you bring me here?" came a woman's voice.

"That's Gwen!" exclaimed Agatha.

"I had to get you somewhere alone. Walt just glares at me."

"And Gareth. What's going on?" wondered Agatha.

She and Toni stood by the trap where they could clearly hear what was going on up on the stage.

"Walt is still furious with John for having dumped me," said Gwen.

"Gwen, you know I've always loved you. Walt will be going off to university. We could get married."

"The last thing I want to think about at the moment is marriage to anyone," said Gwen. "Take me home."

"But say you'll think about it, please," begged Gareth.

"I'll think about it. I must get back or Walt will wonder what's happened to me."

Their voices faded as they left the stage, Gareth still pleading.

"Let's get out of here," said Agatha.

In Toni's car, Agatha said urgently, "We've got to warn Gareth."

"I wouldn't do that," said Toni cautiously.

"Why not? If I'm right about Walt, Gareth could be next on the list."

"He's in love," said Toni. "He'll be furious with you. He'll tell Gwen, who'll tell her son about our nasty suspicions and then you might be the next target."

"I'll think about it," said Agatha huffily, not wanting to tell her young assistant that she was probably right.

CHAPTER TEN

Toni dropped Agatha in Mircester and Agatha got into her own car and drove to her home.

As she got out of her car, Agatha was suddenly aware of a feeling of menace. She stood for a moment, frozen with fear. A car turned into Lilac Lane, illuminating her in its headlights.

The car stopped and Charles got out. Agatha breathed a sigh of relief. This case was getting to her and making her imagine things.

Charles followed her into her cottage. "Shouldn't you be squiring your fiancée?" asked Agatha.

"She sent the ring back."

"Come through to the kitchen while I feed my cats and tell me about it."

"There's nothing to tell. She simply posted the ring back to me."

"And what explanation did she give?"

"I didn't ask. I knew anyway."

"What did you know?"

"That she was following me, that she saw me having dinner with you and no doubt followed me back here and waited to see if I would spend the night."

"So if you knew all that, why the hell did you stay the night?" asked Agatha, taking fish out of the fridge.

He shrugged. "I don't like being spied on. Talk about something else. How's the case?"

"Before I do that," said Agatha. "I'm feeling guilty. It was because of me that your last engagement broke up."

"Well, she was spying as well and I don't like being snooped on. So what's been happening?"

Agatha told him about her visit to the village hall and Gareth's proposal and ended up by saying, "What has that wretched woman got to make all the men dotty about her?"

"Money."

"They're not all like you, Charles."

"Nasty."

"Well, you are awfully mercenary. Any dinner with you and you start croaking like a parrot, 'Oh, I seem to have forgotten my wallet.' Anyway, I think John was after her money, but Gareth does seem to be carrying a torch for her. I wanted to warn him but Toni pointed out it might make me the next target."

"Clever girl. So what now?"

Agatha arranged fish on two plates and put them on the floor. When she straightened up, she said, "I think John's dead body is somewhere. Where would you hide a body?"

Charles groaned. "It could be anywhere — down a well, in a bale of hay, buried six feet deep, lots of places. Forget about it for the evening. Stop brooding over your cats like a mother hen. Let's go through and have a drink and watch some television."

Agatha was suddenly tired. As Charles surfed the channels, trying to find something to watch, she suddenly fell asleep. Charles rose and took a burning cigarette gently from her fingers and stubbed it out in the ashtray.

He found a film of *Sweeney Todd* and settled down comfortably to watch it.

Almost at the end of the musical, Agatha awoke with a jerk. She rubbed her eyes and said, "Sorry. I dropped off. What are you watching?"

"Sweeney Todd."

"Oh, the chap who baked people into pies.

Any good?"

"Not bad. Shut up until I see the end."

Agatha leaned back in her armchair, bits of the Winter Parva murders swirling around in her brain. She began to nod off again. A picture of Pixie rose before her mind's eye. "The steak pie was ever so good," the dream Pixie was saying.

Agatha jerked awake again and stared at Charles. "Snakes and bastards," she said. "Meat pies!"

"You hungry?"

"No. Listen to this. What if Walt got rid of John by cutting up his body and putting it in the steak pies?"

"This musical's been getting into your brain while you were asleep. Anyway how would Walt have the time? The stag party was before the wedding and —"

"And steak pies were served at the reception. He could have been up most of the night. I must get hold of one of those pies," said Agatha. "Let me see. He knows me and Toni. He'll have seen you with me. Phil's been in the village."

"You're nuts," said Charles. "I'm tired. I'm going to bed."

"Oh, shove off, then. You're no help."

"Night, beloved. I'll come and see you in your rubber room."

Agatha phoned Patrick Mulligan. "Patrick," she said, "I want you to get over to the bakery in Winter Parva in the morning and buy a steak pie and bring it to me at the office. I'll explain later."

The next morning when Patrick returned from Winter Parva, she told her staff about her suspicions. Mrs. Freedman sniffed at the pie. "It looks lovely and smells just as it ought."

"Nonetheless, I'm taking it straight to that forensic laboratory in Birmingham and I'll pay them for a rush job. I want them to tell me what the meat is. They'll probably think I'm one of those people who are worried about horsemeat passing off as steak."

Despite Agatha's pleas, she was told the analysis would take a week. But as the days of waiting dragged on, she began to feel silly. Thank goodness she hadn't told them she thought the meat was human flesh.

Two days before the analysis was due, Agatha drove to Carsely and decided to go to the Red Lion for a drink before going home. As she sat in the dark bar, she was almost tempted to book a room for the night. The past few days, she had endured a feeling of dread, almost as if she was being spied on.

Of course, she thought, it could be Charles's fiancée playing detective. Charles had not called and she did not know whether his engagement was on or off.

The long bar was crowded so she took her drink to a table in the corner. A tall, fairly handsome man at the bar turned round and looked at her. Agatha took out her compact but the bar was too dark to make out what she looked like. She picked up her bag but left her drink on the table and hurried to the ladies' room. Agatha quickly repaired her make-up but when she returned to the bar, the good-looking man had gone. She took a gulp of her drink and deciding not to finish it, thought she'd better stop being silly and just go home.

She stood up, her head beginning to swim. Her legs seemed to have turned to jelly. She staggered towards the door and a strong arm went round her waist to support her. As her head continued to swim, she thought it must be the handsome man, but her vision was blurred.

She was thrust into the back of a white van. In a panic, she realised something was badly wrong, but that was her last thought before she fell unconscious.

The next morning, at the agency, her staff

waited in vain for Agatha to arrive. Toni tried her home number and mobile number without success.

Then she phoned Charles. Any phone calls to him were usually blocked by his man, Gustav. But to her relief, it was Charles himself who answered. She quickly told him about her worries about Agatha, and, knowing he had a set of keys to Agatha's cottage, she begged him to go over to Carsely and make sure Agatha was all right.

They all waited anxiously. At last Charles phoned to say Agatha was not at home and there was no sign that her bed had been slept in.

Agatha recovered consciousness. She had been frightened before in her career but never as frightened as this. She was bound and gagged and lying on a pile of flour sacks. She was in some sort of stores cupboard.

Twisting around and struggling at her bonds, Agatha's eyes fell on one shiny black man's shoe. It looked remarkably like the sort of shoes John Hale had worn.

The door opened and Walt Simple walked in. He grinned at Agatha and said, "I'm having a big sale of meat pies tomorrow at the final day of the bakery, and you, you old frump, will be in every one." He kicked her in the side and walked out.

Toni and Patrick went round to police headquarters and demanded to see Bill Wong. They waited and fretted until Bill appeared. He listened in amazement to their tale of the missing Agatha and to Agatha's theory that John Hale had been murdered and made into pies.

"She's been reading too many detective stories," said Bill. "If something has happened to her, it might be Luke Newton. I'll pull him in for questioning."

"No! You've got to get a search warrant and go to that bakery," shouted Toni.

"Agatha sent a meat pie to Birmingham for analysis," said Patrick. "Why don't you phone them?"

"Leave it to me," said Bill. "But Agatha often has these mad flights of fantasy. I'll question Luke first."

Back at the office, Toni said, "We'd better get over to that bakery. We daren't wait."

They set out in their cars only to be stopped on the main road out of Mircester by an overturned truck. They fumed and fretted as the time passed.

Bill and Alice were grilling a sulky Luke Newton. Luke was protesting for the umpteenth time that he had not seen Agatha when the door to the interview room opened and Wilkes summoned Bill. When Bill went out, Wilkes said urgently, "I've just had a call from the lab in Birmingham. There is human flesh in that meat pie. Get rid of young Newton. The sooner we get to that bakery, the better."

Agatha's hands were fastened with plastic cuffs. She rolled around the room, looking for something sharp. Dimly, she heard the noises from the shop. If only she wasn't gagged and could shout. She saw an old scythe propped up in one corner. She rolled towards it and then started to saw at one of the cuffs on her wrist.

It was slow and agonising work but extreme fear had leant her strength. At last, the cuff fell apart. Agatha unfastened the other one and then ripped the tape from her mouth.

She unfastened the ropes that bound her ankles and stood up shakily and tottered to the door.

It was locked. The noises from the shop had ceased. Agatha looked at her watch. Lunch time. Probably the bakery was closed.

She heard footsteps approaching and hid behind the door.

The room was dark. Walt walked in and strode towards the pile of flour sacks on the floor. He swung round just in time to see Agatha darting out the door.

With a cry of rage, he ran after her. Agatha ran into the bakery shop. She seized a large meat pie and threw it straight into Walt's face. He clawed the meat off. Agatha grabbed more meat pies and threw them as she made towards the door. The door was locked. She let out a whimper of fear and Walt approached her, his eyes blazing with hate. "Help," said Agatha weakly. And then gathering all her strength, she screamed, "Help!" at the top of her voice.

Charles had joined Agatha's staff as they arrived at the bakery in time to hear that scream.

Patrick took a cosh out of his pocket and broke the glass on the doors, put his hand in and turned the key. The sound of sirens coming along the street could be heard behind them.

They all burst in to hear Agatha shouting, "He's getting away. Round the back!"

The police arrived in time to hear Agatha's shout and raced to the back of the bakery.

Charles gathered Agatha into his arms. She was shaking from head to foot. "There, now," he said. "It's all over."

But Walt had disappeared. They searched the bakery without success and then the whole area round about. Gwen arrived from a shopping expedition and was taken into custody.

The whole village seemed to have gathered outside the bakery. There was to be an investigation later to find out which gabby policeman had told the villagers what was in the meat pies. Several began to vomit and others clutched their stomachs. The crowd began to disperse to form a queue outside the doctor's surgery instead.

Bill said to Agatha, "You'd better come with us for questioning."

"I can't," wailed Agatha. "I've peed myself."

"We'll find you clean clothes," said Bill.

Agatha arrived at police headquarters and learned that Gwen had collapsed and had been taken to hospital.

Before the questioning began, a bag was

handed in. Agatha was told Charles had gone to her cottage and had packed up a set of clean clothes. She was allowed a break while she donated a urine sample and got washed and changed.

Wilkes was furious. How the hell did this woman with no real detective training leap to the conclusion that the late John Hale was in the meat pies?

Wearily, Agatha described how she had finished a drink at the George, had felt dizzy, her vision was too blurred to see who was helping her out of the hotel and the next thing she knew, she was trussed up in the bakery.

At the end of the interview, Agatha was told a police guard would be put outside her cottage, but she said she was going back just to deliver her cats to Doris Simpson and then she was going to stay at the George Hotel.

Later that day, she was to learn through Patrick that a forensic team had found a trapdoor in the floor of one of the freezers leading to a tunnel which exited in the back lane outside. It was guessed that Walt had hidden down there until he felt it safe to make his escape.

■ ■ ■ ■

A media frenzy enveloped Winter Parva for days. Pixie got her photograph on the front page of the local paper, saying that she and John had once been betrothed. That was subsequently found out to be a lie but Pixie did not care. She had enjoyed her moment of glory. Agatha gave interview after interview, much to the fury of Wilkes, who had been trying to claim that the discovery of John Hale's macabre death had been the result of police work.

Agatha took that week off work to recover. She had a large bruise in her side where Walt had kicked her and her wrist had bruises where the cuffs had bit into them.

She grew extremely fond of Charles, who called daily to sit and talk nonsense and cheer her up.

Meanwhile, the search for Walt Simple spread throughout the country and abroad. A hot line was set up. Reports of sightings came from all over and were followed up but without any of them leading to finding Walt.

On the second last day of her stay at the George, Agatha went down to the bar for a preluncheon drink. The first thing she saw was that nearly handsome man at the bar. She had an impulse to join him at the bar instead of sitting down at one of the tables and waiting to give her order to one of the staff, but memories of all the mistakes she had made in the past, ending up with Paul Newton, crowded into her brain, and so she meekly took herself to a table in the corner.

She ordered a gin and tonic, wishing she could smoke. Charles would probably call on her soon. Dear Charles.

"Mrs. Raisin? It is Mrs. Agatha Raisin, is it not?"

Agatha looked up and blinked. The nearly handsome man was smiling down at her.

"That's me," said Agatha.

"I read about you in the newspapers. You are a very brave lady."

Agatha smiled up at him. "Won't you join me?"

"I'll just get my drink."

Agatha quickly flipped open her compact. Make-up all right. Damn! There was a little hair at the side of her mouth.

He came back and sat down.

"It must have been awful for you," he said. "I haven't introduced myself. I'm Jeremy Rutherford."

"I'm getting over it," said Agatha. "Are you a resident of Mircester?"

"No, I live in Walton Magna. It's a few miles outside Mircester to the south."

"And what do you do in Walton Magna?"

"I have an antique shop."

"Have you always been an antique dealer?"

"No, I was in the army for years. Finished my army career two years ago."

"So why antiques?"

"My father was a collector. He died two years ago and left me a house crammed with antiques along with his antique shop. At first I was going to put stuff up for auction, but I thought it would be fun to carry on the business and get rid of some of the stuff that was cluttering up the house at the same time. What about you? How did you get into the detective business?"

Agatha began to happily brag about her career until he interrupted her by saying, "Why don't we continue this conversation in the dining room?"

Out of the gloom of the bar and in the bright light of the dining room, Agatha covertly studied her companion. He had thick brown hair streaked with grey, a pleasant square face, a firm mouth and a good figure.

Charles stood at the entrance to the dining

room. He was about to join Agatha and her companion, but Agatha looked so happy and animated that he turned and went back into the bar instead. He felt Agatha needed something to take her mind off her recent horrible experience. He'd find out who this man was later.

After lunch, Agatha trailed up to her room, disappointed. Jeremy had not suggested they meet again. Probably married, she thought wistfully. He had been in the army and had known James. She resolved to see if James could tell her more about him.

She was supposed to tell the police when she was returning to her cottage so they could put a police guard on her door, but she was sick of the police. She felt Bill Wong should at least have called on her and Wilkes had treated her as if she were the criminal.

Agatha checked out of the hotel. She sat in her car, took a pair of tweezers out of her handbag and pulled that little hair out. She was amazed to see how tiny it was. During the meal with Jeremy, she had been too conscious of that offending hair, feeling it growing in size. She had been frightened to escape to the ladies' room to deal with it in case Jeremy might be joined by people he knew. You silly cow, Agatha chastised herself as she drove to Carsely. If by any chance some friend had joined him, then you might have found out whether he was married.

She had phoned her cleaner, Doris Simpson, before she had left the hotel and Doris promised to take Agatha's cats back to her cottage.

Agatha let herself into her cottage to a rare welcome from her cats, who usually punished her by ignoring her when she had been away.

She sat down on the kitchen floor and petted them, feeling the tears beginning to run down her cheeks. Agatha wanted a strong man to turn up, to take her in his arms and tell her he would look after her until the end of time. She wondered whether she would ever have the courage to go on detecting.

She got to her feet and dried her eyes. It was a beautiful spring day. She let the cats out into the garden, sat down on a chair at the garden table and let out a long slow sigh of relief. A cherry tree lifted its heavy pink blossoms up to the clear sky. Agatha employed a woman gardener. The lawn was covered in crocuses and daffodils nodded on the borders. A blackbird poured liquid song down from the rooftops. It was like falling off a tall building and suddenly discovering that you had not broken any bones, thought Agatha. Life was all right.

CHAPTER ELEVEN

Agatha phoned Bill Wong to say she was back at her cottage. Bill reported the fact to Wilkes and said they should send a police guard but Wilkes was furious with Agatha for having had so much publicity in the newspapers. He felt she had made the police look stupid and so he told Bill there would be no police guard because Walt would not dare show his face in the Cotswolds again. In vain did Bill point out that a man who was so obsessed with his mother that he should bump off her fiancé would surely try to see Gwen again and maybe get revenge on Agatha. So Agatha learned that she was to have no protection.

But the glorious weather continued. One sunny day followed another. The lilac tree in Agatha's front garden bowed down under a heavy weight of blossom.

Jeremy had not phoned although she had given him her card. Had he phoned immediately after their lunch, Agatha might have considered whether she was really interested. But like all immature romantics, she was addicted to the hunt, building up dream pictures of a man she barely knew. Charles was again absent and James Lacey still abroad, and without a man around, Agatha felt diminished.

Also, she needed something to take her mind off the fact that Walt had not been found.

Roy came down one week-end, complaining that he had been tied up with a PR account when Agatha was getting all the publicity. To Agatha's amazement, her former employee's craving for self-publicity had actually made him jealous of her. He had not told her he was coming and she was tempted to tell him she had too much to do to entertain him, but she was lonely.

Somewhere at the back of her mind was the uneasy thought that a modern business-woman like herself should be self-sufficient. Agatha asked Roy why he was so conservatively dressed, as he usually wore something outrageous. He was wearing a tweed jacket and cords over a checked shirt.

"I've been publicising that fishing tackle shop, Angler's Dream. I tell you, I've become fascinated by the idea of fishing and even took a couple of lessons in fly fishing. I've got a treat for you. I've two rods in the car. Why don't we go fishing?"

"I don't know anything about it."

"I'll show you," said Roy eagerly. "I stopped off in Mircester and got a couple of fishing permits for the upper reaches of the Mir. It would be fun."

Agatha hesitated only a moment. It was another lovely day.

"All right," she said. "I'll watch you."

"I've even got the Luxury Fisherman's Picnic Hamper. They made me a present of it."

"Sounds fine," said Agatha. "Let's go."

They settled themselves on the bank of the river. There were a few anglers wearing waders out in the middle of the river.

"Why don't they just sit on the bank and be comfortable like us?" asked Agatha.

She was soon to find out when Roy started fishing. The banks of the river were lined with trees and he caught his hook in branches and spent ages trying to dislodge it.

"Don't you have waders like those other chaps?" asked Agatha.

"I've got some in the car," said Roy sulkily. "But I can't swim."

"The water's shallow," said Agatha. "It's only just up above their knees."

Roy went to the car and came back with the waders. "Let's eat first," he said.

The picnic was very good and there was even a bottle of wine. "The effects of the alcohol will have worn off by the time we drive back," said Agatha.

"It'll still show up on a breathalyser," Roy pointed out. "And you're driving."

"Okay. I'll have one glass."

While they ate, the sun went in and a little breeze sent ripples over the river.

"Maybe we should go back," said Agatha. "It's getting cold."

"Better weather for fishing," said Roy.

While Agatha packed away the picnic debris, Roy pulled on his waders, picked up his rod and gingerly walked into the river. The first thing he discovered was that the other anglers must be tall because the water came up to the top of his hips. There was quite a strong current.

His first catch was another angler who cursed him roundly as Roy detached his hook from the man's jacket and apologised profusely.

"Get away from me, you little faggot," roared the man.

"I'll sue you!" shouted Roy. "That's slander."

On the riverbank, Agatha sighed and wished she had not come. Then she was plagued with a feeling of menace. She twisted round but could not see anything lurking in the trees.

Roy had caught something on his line. His face was pink with excitement as he began to reel it in.

There was the sound of a gunshot and at the same time Roy fell facedown into the river.

Agatha kicked off her shoes and plunged into the river, shouting, "Get the police, he's been shot."

The anglers and Agatha pulled Roy upright. "Have you been hit?" asked Agatha.

"Hit with what?" gasped Roy. "Some damned fish pulled me over and it's made off with my rod."

"Get out of this river," said Agatha. "Someone just tried to shoot you." She turned to the other anglers. "Don't leave, any of you. I'm calling the police."

The police arrived very quickly and began to search through the trees.

Agatha and Roy were soaking wet.

Four anglers stood around them, waiting impatiently. Said one to Roy, "Your mother's imagination has just ruined a day's fishing."

"I did not imagine it!" howled Agatha. "And he is not my son."

The two policemen who had originally arrived had been joined by others.

And then to Agatha's relief, Bill Wong and Alice Peterson appeared.

"You were right," said Bill. "We've just found a shotgun cartridge. Maybe someone was shooting at you and it went over your head." He turned to the anglers. "I'll need you to give me your names and addresses after I have taken your statements. Agatha, you and Roy can go and change into dry clothes and report to police headquarters. A police car will escort you back."

As soon as they were in the car with the heater blasting, Roy took out his mobile phone.

"Put that thing away," ordered Agatha. "I've had enough of the press."

Roy had a change of clothes, as he meant to stay overnight. As soon as he was in the spare room, he took out his mobile and began to phone every newspaper and television station he could think of until Agatha shouted that the police were waiting to take them to Mircester.

■ ■ ■ ■

Agatha and Roy were interviewed separately. This time, Agatha was interviewed not only by Wilkes, but by a Detective Superintendent Bloggs. He was a large grey lump of man in a baggy suit. Agatha thought his name suited him.

She was taken over the events bit by bit and then Bloggs said, "We're wondering whether he was shooting at you. It could be Walt Simple trying to take revenge."

"I swear Roy was the target for some reason," said Agatha. "He was down the river and a good bit away to my left. It couldn't have been Walt. Why try to kill Roy?"

"Mr. Silver is very effeminate," said Bloggs. "Is he gay?"

"I don't know," said Agatha. "Anyway, what's that got to do with anything?"

"It may have nothing to do with Simple," said Bloggs. "Do you know if Mr. Silver has a lover?"

"I don't. And if he had, he would hardly want to spend a week-end with me."

"What is your relationship with Mr. Silver?"

"He's an ex-employee, not a friend."

"Are you sure?"

"Look," said Agatha wearily, "I'm old enough to be his mother."

"Doesn't mean you aren't having an affair," said Bloggs.

"I'm off!" Agatha got to her feet. "I'm not going to sit here any longer listening to your rubbish."

When Agatha had left, Wilkes said, "We'd better put a police guard on her."

But Bloggs was furious with Agatha. She had not treated him with the deference he was used to. "Let her rot," he said savagely.

"But if it was Simple who was after her," protested Wilkes, "and we keep a watch on her, we might catch the murdering bastard."

But Bloggs, whose nickname was the Walking Ego, would not be moved.

To Roy's dismay, they were ushered out of the back of the police station to avoid the press. Worse was to come for Roy, because Agatha told the police not to go near her cottage but to drop them both at the vicarage.

Mrs. Bloxby ushered her into her comfortable living room and listened in horror to Agatha's account of the shooting. Roy chewed his nails and fretted.

"I'll get us all a nice glass of sherry," said

Mrs. Bloxby.

"May I use your bathroom?" asked Roy.

"Of course. You know where it is."

Roy went into the bathroom and locked the door. As he had remembered, the frosted glass window opened out into the church-yard. He opened it and climbed out and fled through the churchyard and did not stop running until he had reached Agatha's cottage to confront the waiting press. He happily gave interview after interview.

Agatha would have preferred a gin and tonic but sherry and the vicarage seemed to go together. The vicar came into the room. "Who's in the bathroom?"

"Mr. Silver," said his wife.

"I keep rattling the handle but he won't open the door."

"Maybe he's constipated," said Mrs. Bloxby.

"*I'm* not!" shouted the vicar. "You, Mrs. Raisin, get him out of there now!"

Followed by the vicar and his wife, Agatha went to the bathroom door and rattled the handle and shouted, "Are you all right?"

Silence.

"I'll kill that little toad," said the vicar. He went off and came back with a chisel, which he inserted in the doorjamb and wrenched.

The door cracked open. No Roy, but they immediately saw the window was opened.

"He's gone to meet the press," said Agatha. "Well, he's welcome to them."

"Do you mind clearing off and letting me use the toilet?" said the vicar. "Mrs. Raisin, I'll send you the bill for whatever it costs to repair the door."

"Doesn't he ever practise Christian forgiveness?" demanded Agatha crossly, as she and Mrs. Bloxby retreated to the living room.

"Not when he has trouble with his bowels," said Mrs. Bloxby. "Now, wasn't the name of that farmer Paul Newton?"

"Yes."

"There was an announcement in yesterday's paper that he is getting married."

"Who to?" asked Agatha.

"To a Caroline Featherington."

"Dear me. She was Charles's fiancée. I wonder what he thinks about that? She was spying on Charles which is why she broke off the engagement. She saw me having dinner with him and then he spent the night. That's the second time that has happened. I feel guilty."

"You shouldn't," said the vicar's wife. "If Sir Charles had really wanted to marry her, he would have brought her to meet you and all would have been explained. Anyone in your life at the moment?"

"Not a soul. I do hope Walt Simple isn't planning to murder me. But why would he try to kill Roy?"

"Perhaps he thought Roy was your son and thought that would hurt you dreadfully."

"Could be," said Agatha. "But I can't help hoping the police find it was some nut case who had nothing to do with the Winter Parva murders."

"Would you like to stay here for the night?" asked Mrs. Bloxby.

But before Agatha could reply, they heard the vicar saying, "Bloody woman!" and slamming the door of his office behind him.

"Honestly," said Agatha crossly. "If I'm ever in church and hear your husband preaching about forgiveness and charity I shall heckle him."

She went down to her cottage. She ignored both Roy and the press, went in and up to the spare room. She packed Roy's overnight bag, went back down, opened the door, placed it on the step and retreated before a barrage of questions from the press.

As Agatha went into the kitchen, her phone rang. She decided to answer it, knowing that the press did not have her ex-directory number. It was Roy.

"Couldn't I just come in and explain things?" pleaded Roy. "The press want a picture of us together."

Agatha slammed down the phone.

She suddenly wanted something to take her mind off murder and mayhem.

The next day was a beautiful Saturday. She fed her cats and let them out into the garden. The air was redolent with the scent of flowers. A white clematis with blooms the size of dinner plates hung over the door.

What was the name of that village where Jeremy had his antiques shop? Walton Magna, that was it. She went inside and collected her iPad, took it out to the garden and searched for directions to Walton Magna.

Agatha went upstairs and changed into a cotton dress that had a low neckline and a short skirt. She put on a pair of high-heeled strapped sandals. She then put on a dark blue raw silk jacket, checked her make-up, and went down to brave the press who were still lurking outside her door.

"I am sure Roy Silver has told you all you need to know," she said firmly. She thrust her way through them, got into her car and drove off.

She parked at the side of the road on the outskirts of Walton Magna and wondered whether to turn round and go home. But she had seen nothing of a police guard and home meant worrying that Walt Simple was advancing on her.

She drove on into the village and easily located the shop, for Walton Magna was little more than a hamlet. Rutherford Antiques was the only shop in the village.

The supermarkets and the motorcar had killed off most of the village shops. Agatha could see evidence of where shops had once been, now turned into cottages.

She looked in the window of the shop to see if there was anything she would like to buy.

A ghostly Agatha Raisin looked back at her from her reflection in the window.

She wanted to turn away and go home. But what if she had been seen? It would look odd.

Agatha took a deep breath, pushed open the door and went in. The shop appeared to be empty. She looked at the ornaments, at the clocks, at the furniture and then saw in a corner a tall pier glass mirror with a carved gilt frame. I could put that in my bedroom, thought Agatha. The mirror in the bathroom only shows me from the waist up.

"Can I help you?"

Agatha started and swung round. An elegant young man was standing there. He was small and neat, wearing a white shirt and white trousers. His hair was fair and his eyes large and grey and tilted slightly at the corners.

"How much is that mirror?" asked Agatha.

"It's George the Third," he said. "Attributed to George Cole. It's valued at ten thousand pounds."

"Blimey. Can't you come down a bit?"

"I'm not the boss. You'd need to ask Mr. Rutherford."

"I know Mr. Rutherford," said Agatha. "We had lunch together. Is he here?"

"He stepped out for a minute."

"I'll have a look for something else," said Agatha. "I'm afraid I can't afford the mirror."

"I'll leave you to it. Shout if you want me."

"You're very trusting. What if I nick something?"

"We've security cameras all over the place. Knock yourself out."

He grinned and waved. Soon Agatha could hear the sound of an Australian soap coming from the back shop.

Agatha felt suddenly tired. He looks like Puck, she thought, and that rhymes with . . .

"Oh, hullo, Jeremy."

"Agatha! How nice to see you again. Did you come to see me or did you want an antique?"

"Both," said Agatha.

"And what are you looking for?"

Agatha looked wildly around until her eye fell on a brass coal scuttle. "That scuttle would look nice on my hearth. How much?"

"It's eighty pounds. I'll let you have it for sixty. It's modern. Do you want me to wrap it up?"

"Don't bother. It's got a handle."

Agatha paid by debit card and picked up the scuttle.

"Have you had lunch?"

"No."

"I know a nice pub near here."

"My treat," said Agatha. "You paid for the last lunch."

"Leave the scuttle. You can get it on your road back. Going out, Perry!" he shouted.

"Okay," came an answering call.

Jeremy helped Agatha into his BMW and they drove off. They came to a pub called the Jolly Farmer.

"They've got tables in the garden," said Jeremy.

"Good," commented Agatha. "That means I can smoke."

"You actually smoke," he said. "I thought nobody smoked these days."

"Just me and the other dinosaurs," said Agatha crossly.

The pub garden was sunny and delicious smells of cooking wafted from the kitchen.

The sun was quite strong so they found a table in the shade of a large cedar.

Agatha sighed with pleasure as she studied the menu. "Oh, good. They've got roast beef and Yorkshire pudding. I won't need a starter."

The waitress came up. Jeremy ordered a half of lager for himself and a gin and tonic for Agatha. "I think we're ready to order our food as well. The lady will have the roast beef and I will have the spinach quiche and salad. And we'll have a bottle of Merlot. Now," he said, when the waitress had left, "you've been in the wars again."

Agatha told him briefly what had happened without her usual embellishments and exaggerations.

He looked around anxiously as if to see an assassin lurking behind the trees.

"Are you sure he won't try again?" he asked.

"I hope not," said Agatha. "Tell me about

yourself. How did you meet James?"

He talked about his experiences in Iraq and how James had been his colonel. He had a husky, pleasant voice. Agatha began to relax. The food when it came was excellent. While he talked on, Agatha began to dream of marriage. No more frights or attempts on her life.

But when the meal was over and he drove her back to her car, he had said nothing about wanting to see her again.

Before she got in her car, Agatha said, "May I take you for lunch one day next week?"

He hesitated. "I've a lot to do. I'll phone you."

Feeling crushed, Agatha drove off. She realised she hadn't even asked him if he were married.

But as she drove into Lilac Lane, she saw with a lifting of her heart that James Lacey's car was parked on the street outside his cottage. She stopped abruptly, got out and rang his doorbell.

"Agatha!" exclaimed James. "Welcome. I've been reading about you. Come in."

Settling happily on the sofa while James went to make her a coffee, Agatha reflected that having James back next door gave her a much-needed feeling of security.

When he came back with her coffee, she said, "I've just been having lunch with Jeremy Rutherford. Evidently, he knows you."

"Oh, him. I actually don't know him very well. I bumped into him in Mircester a couple of days before our wedding. I knew him in Iraq. We had a drink and talked a bit."

"Is he married?"

"I don't know. Still husband hunting, Agatha? Weren't two marriages enough for you?"

"I am not husband hunting!"

"Never mind," said James. "Tell me all about your adventures."

So Agatha did, although she felt she had been talking about them so much recently that her own voice seemed to belong to someone else.

When she had finished, James looked worried. "I've a feeling he'll try to get you again. Why isn't there a policeman outside your door?"

"I don't know. Although Wilkes is so furious with me, he probably hopes I will get bumped off."

James rose and began to pace up and down the room. "Look, Agatha," he said at last. "You'd better move in here and bring your cats."

Agatha surveyed his handsome face and figure, thinking ruefully of the days when such an invitation would have sent her to seventh heaven.

But such security would be a relief. "All right," she said.

"Give me your car keys. I'll park your car somewhere out of sight," said James. "You go and pack. I'll be along in a short time to carry the cat boxes for you."

Agatha had forgotten just how fussy James was. She had to make sure that she always put a coaster under her coffee or wineglass. She slept in the spare room. The bed was not only covered by a duvet but a top sheet as well and that top sheet was firmly anchored. She had wrenched it loose and thrown it on the floor only to find it back on the bed later the next morning.

James settled down to work after breakfast. Agatha switched on the television and James told her to switch it off because the noise was too distracting. Agatha took a Kindle out of her handbag and turned it on.

James glanced up. "I'm shocked you have one of those, Agatha. Don't you ever think of the poor booksellers being put out of business by these electronic monsters?"

"I have plenty of real books in my cottage," said Agatha huffily. "Go back to your work and leave me alone."

Agatha began to read a new detective story. The plot was going along nicely until Agatha got to the bit where the hero was estranged from his father and he was telling his lady love all about his dysfunctional childhood. "Pah!" said Agatha.

"Pah what?" asked James, looking up.

"It's happening in books and on television," complained Agatha. "The hero always has issues with his father, and in television series, you just know there's going to be a long cheesy bit where they get round to the reconciliation. Of course it saves the script writers a lot of words as father and son gaze into each other's eyes in silence accompanied by an angel choir."

"You had a rotten upbringing," said James, who had heard about Agatha's drunken parents.

"Yes, but I moved on," said Agatha impatiently. "Oh, well, I've started this story so I may as well read the damn thing."

But the book could not hold Agatha's attention. She went up to the spare room and collected her iPad and took it out into the garden, letting her cats out at the same time. She sat down at the garden table and downloaded an old James Bond movie with Sean Connery in the lead.

Her mobile phone rang just as Bond was confronting Blofeld. It was Toni. "Where are you?" she asked.

"I'm staying at James's place."

"I'd like to see you," said Toni. "I'm outside your cottage."

Agatha reluctantly switched off the movie. "Come along."

"It's Toni," said Agatha, walking past James to the front door. And that's made him switch off his computer, thought Agatha jealously, remembering when James had had a crush on Toni.

"So what brings you?" asked Agatha, sourly noticing Toni's attractive outfit of shorts and white blouse.

"I've been thinking," said Toni. "Walt must be obsessed with his mother in some sick way or he wouldn't have killed John Hale and in such a macabre and horrible way. I read your report. Those meat pies were served at the reception. Did he feed one to his mother?"

"Or did his mother know about it?" said Agatha.

"The thing is," said Toni eagerly, "that I cannot see Walt hiding out and not trying to get in touch with his mother. The police won't expect him to go back to the bakery. So why don't we go over after dark and see if we can see anything?"

"It may be dangerous," protested James.

"It's surely more dangerous to leave Agatha like a tethered goat, waiting for Walt to attack."

"All right," said Agatha. "We'll go after dark."

That evening, the three of them crept along the dark lane at the back of the bakery. James located a high wooden door. It was fastened by a large padlock. He took a ring of skeleton keys out of his pocket and got to work. It took him twenty minutes to pick the lock.

They found themselves in a backyard where piles of discarded junk lay in heaps.

James turned round and whispered to Agatha, "You should stand by the back gate on lookout and I and Toni will see if we can hear anything from the bakery."

"Why me?" asked Agatha.

"Oh, don't argue."

Agatha retreated sulkily to the gate.

The village had old-fashioned lights in the main street so there was no orange sodium glare to blot out the stars. It was a beautiful, tranquil evening.

Then she became aware of a feeling of menace. She decided to go and join James and Toni. She was just going forwards when something cold and metallic was pressed against her neck and a voice in her ear said, "You will do exactly what you are told or I will blow your brains out."

Agatha nodded dumbly.

"Shout out loudly that you are going home. Do it!"

Agatha called out, "I'm going home!"

At the back of the house, James cursed. Lights came on at the back of the bakery and Gwen's voice could be heard calling, "Who's there?"

James and Toni crouched down behind two large bins. A door opened and the light from a powerful torch played across the garden. Toni shivered and worried. Agatha's voice had sounded peculiar. At last the torch was switched off and they could hear the back door close.

They hurried down the garden. No Agatha stood at the gate. At first they assumed she had gone into hiding when she had heard Gwen's voice. They ran up and down the lane, calling, "Agatha!" in soft voices, and then, throwing caution to the winds, yelled her name out.

"Something awful has happened," said

Toni. "I'm calling the police."

Agatha had been forced into a wheelie bin, which was tipped over and rolled onto a wheelbarrow. Her mouth had been taped shut. Her hands and feet were bound. She had caught a frightened glimpse of Walt's face before being incarcerated in the bin.

Soon she was conscious of the bin being wheeled upwards. Doors were slammed shut and then the sound of an engine starting up.

Whatever vehicle she was in seemed to drive through the night for a long time.

Exhausted with fear, she nearly fell asleep when the vehicle came to an abrupt stop and she could hear the sound of rushing water.

The falls on the River Mir, thought Agatha. He's going to tip me over.

She heard the doors at the back open and then felt herself being wheeled out.

Agatha made strangled sounds of distress behind her gag and kicked against the sides of the bin.

Walt wheeled the bin to the edge of the bridge over the falls.

He heard a man shout, "Here! You! You can't dump stuff in the river."

Walt swung round and saw a man who

had been walking his dog, staring at him. Heaving the bin over, Walt turned round and raised his gun.

Before he could fire, the dog, a powerful Alsatian, leapt for his throat. Walt was driven back against the low parapet of the bridge and sent flying over into the falls. A bullet fired from his gun shot harmlessly into the air.

He went down and down. His head struck a rock and his body whirled round and round into the pool below the falls and slowly sank.

Above, on the bridge, the dog owner called the police.

The bin survived the falls and sailed lazily round in the pool below. Just as it was about to sink, a little current carried it over to the bank and it wedged under the bank of a willow tree.

Inside the bin, Agatha shivered and prayed. She was sure that any moment now, Walt would descend and put a bullet through the bin. She had heard that shot and assumed Walt had shot the man who had accosted him.

Police were scouring the village of Winter Parva and the surrounding countryside. A police helicopter hovered overhead. Wilkes was furious. He knew there would be an enquiry as to why he had not given Agatha police protection.

Gwen had been interviewed and had said through her tears that she had not seen her son.

James and Toni had been joined by Simon, Patrick and Phil. Suddenly they heard Wilkes shout something and the police cars stared to race off.

"Let's follow them!" shouted Toni.

As someone once pointed out, there are no agnostics on the battlefield. Slumped in the bottom of the bin, Agatha started to do deals with the God she never quite believed in. She was just saying, "If you get me out of this, I'll never smoke again," when she heard the sound of police sirens. Car doors slammed. She could soon hear bodies crashing down through the undergrowth. Agatha made frantic moaning sounds from behind her gag.

A man's voice said, "Get a knife. The lid of the bin's shut. Are you in there, Mrs. Raisin?"

Frantic mumbles from Agatha.

The lid was lifted and concerned police faces looked down. The bin was heaved up onto the bank and tilted on its side. Agatha screamed in pain as she was pulled out. "I think I've broken something," she gasped as soon as her gag was removed and her feet and wrists untied.

She was placed on a stretcher and carried up to a waiting ambulance. Before she was loaded in, Wilkes glared down at her and shouted, "You stupid woman. It's all your own fault."

"Now, then," said Bloggs, pulling him away. "That's enough of that. We've got Simple."

"Are you sure?" gasped Agatha. "What if he escapes?"

"He won't," said Bloggs. "He's dead."

"Thank God," said Agatha Raisin.

EPILOGUE

It turned out that Agatha had two broken ribs. She got herself moved to a private room at the hospital, observing cynically that there was a police guard outside now that she did not need one. She did not know that the police guard was there to stop any members of the press from interviewing her.

One of her visitors was Roy Silver, who, Charles informed her later, was holding press conferences outside the hospital.

"What I wonder," said Agatha to Mrs. Bloxby when the vicar's wife called, "is why Walt went to all that elaborate business of taking me up to the falls."

"He wanted you to suffer. He thought of you as rubbish to be disposed of. His murders were always elaborate."

"I sometimes wonder if I should retire and let Toni run the agency," said Agatha.

"You'd get bored quickly," said Mrs. Bloxby. "But why don't you take a holiday somewhere?"

"I might. I've had lots of visitors, except for Jeremy Rutherford."

"And who is Mr. Rutherford?"

"He runs an antique shop. We had a couple of meals together. Oh, well, he's obviously not interested. I'll be glad to get home. They are releasing me tomorrow. My ribs are strapped up. In fact, I wonder why they keep me in here so long."

"Perhaps the police don't want you to leave until the press have lost interest," said Mrs. Bloxby.

"What I cannot understand," said Agatha, "is why Gwen has not been charged with anything, or so Patrick tells me. I mean, wasn't she around when her son was cutting up a dead body? At least Jed is now only charged with Crosswith's murder. They've got Walt for the murder of Hale and they're pretty sure he killed his father and George Southern."

"My husband was called over to comfort Mrs. Simple," said Mrs Bloxby. "She's in a terrible state. You see, they always made their own meat pies. A carcase would be delivered from the butcher and cut up at the bakery. Walt, like his father, was trained how to butcher meat. She said that latterly she left all the baking and pie making to her

298

son."

"I think she's a slimy, devious woman," said Agatha, "and I bet she knew something."

"Let's hope not," said Mrs. Bloxby. "Have you seen Sir Charles or Mr. Lacey?"

"Yes, that nearly finished basket of fruit is from James. It's nearly finished because Charles ate most of it. Oh, I would like to go home."

"I'll wait until you see a doctor and find out if it's all right," said Mrs. Bloxby. "Then I can drive you home."

Later that day, Agatha sat in Mrs. Bloxby's little car as the vicar's wife drove her down the green lanes to Carsely. The day was sultry with great black clouds looming up in the west.

Agatha refused to go to the vicarage, saying she would be all right on her own. The fact was that she craved a cigarette, although she remembered uneasily promising God to give up smoking if she were saved.

Her cleaner had delivered her cats. Agatha sat down on the floor and patted them. She found her hands were beginning to shake. She still had nightmares about her brush with death. She let the cats out into the garden, made herself a cup of strong black coffee and went and sat at the garden table.

Opening a packet of Bensons, Agatha lit a cigarette. A great flash of forked lightning stabbed down, followed by a drum roll of thunder.

Agatha was struck by superstitious dread. She hurriedly stubbed out the cigarette as the rain came down in sheets and her cats scampered indoors for shelter.

There was a pile of mail on the kitchen table. Agatha sat down and flicked through it. One large square envelope caught her eye. She opened it up.

At first she thought it was a wedding invitation but on reading the curly embossed script, she found it was an invitation from Jeremy Rutherford to a party at his home. She quickly checked the date. The party was due to take place in three days' time on Saturday evening.

All Agatha's fears left her as she began to plan what to wear.

In the next few days, she was too busy getting her face done at the beautician's and her hair freshly tinted to wonder overmuch why James had not called on her.

By Saturday, the weather was glorious again. Agatha set out wearing a scarlet silk chiffon dress cut on the bias so that it seemed to float around her when she walked.

Jeremy Rutherford's house turned out to be a large Georgian building set in its own grounds. There were a lot of cars already parked outside the mansion. Someone rapped on her window as she hesitated, wondering where to find a space. She lowered the window to find herself confronted by a young man wearing a parking attendant's hat, a black leather thong, high boots and nothing else.

"There's a space over there beside that Jag," he said politely.

Agatha moved her car into the space. He might have told me it was fancy dress, she thought.

She went into the house. There were two rooms off a large square hall and all seemed to be filled with men. There were men over at a buffet in the hall, men in one of the rooms dancing together, men hugging each other, and a few women. Oh, no, thought Agatha. They're not women, they're men in drag.

Jeremy emerged from the crowd. He was wearing a black T-shirt and tight black trousers. "Listen up, folks!" he shouted. "This is the famous Agatha Raisin you've all read about."

Faces crowded around Agatha. They're all looking at me as if I were some strange beast, thought Agatha.

"Jeremy," she said firmly, "this is not my scene and you should have known that. I don't want to be on display."

She turned and marched out the door, followed by cries of, "Ooh! Temper. Temper."

Jeremy caught up with her as she was getting into her car. "I'm sorry, Agatha. Do come back in. Everyone's dying to meet you."

"Maybe another time," said Agatha, and drove off.

She found Charles waiting for her when she arrived home. He laughed when she told him about the party. "Antiques, Agatha. You should have known."

"No, I shouldn't," snapped Agatha. "I know a lot of heterosexual antique dealers. I might have stayed if it hadn't been obvious that he'd only invited me along as some sort of curiosity. What a waste! A lot of the fellows were very good-looking."

"How are you feeling now that you're home?" asked Charles.

"A bit shaky but I'll get over it. Gareth Craven sent a large cheque. I'm still bothered about Gwen."

"Yes, she got off, didn't she?"

"If mother and son were so unhealthily close as to make Walt want to bump off her fiancé, then it stands to reason she must have known something. Stop reading my mail."

"I like reading other people's mail. So much more interesting than mine. Oh, look at this. Carsely's got its own therapist. Maybe you should go."

"Let me see. Jill Davent, qualified therapist. Leave your troubles with me. Yack, yack, yack. Bound to be a charlatan."

"Why do you say that?"

"She's working from home. Ivy Cottage."

"Forget her. Want to go and see Gwen?"

"She won't see me," said Agatha.

"She'll see me. I'll bet she's on the hunt for a husband now that her possessive son is out of the road."

"May as well," said Agatha. "I'm still curious."

Winter Parva lay innocently before them in the soft twilight as they drove into the village. "You'd never think there had been murder and mayhem going on here," said Agatha.

"You'd better wait in the car," said Charles. "She won't let us in if she sees you."

"Oh, all right," said Agatha. "I wish I'd brought a book."

Gareth Craven answered the door to Charles. To Charles's request to see Gwen, he said, "Poor Gwen is not seeing anyone but me."

Gwen appeared beside Gareth. "Why, Sir Charles! Do come in."

How can she bear to go on living here? wondered Charles. He walked through to the back shop. The living quarters were on the right at the end of a long dim passage and to the back were, he assumed, where the freezers and the room that had been Agatha's prison.

"I came to see how you were getting on," said Charles.

"Do sit down," said Gwen. "We were just about to have tea. Gareth, dear, don't you have something to do?"

"No," said Gareth sulkily, sitting down opposite Charles.

Gwen waited until she had served tea and then smiled at Charles. "I'm moving out tomorrow. The wine company is moving in."

Charles looked around the kitchen. "Nothing seems to be packed," he said.

"Oh, I'm paying for one of these super duper removal firms. They do it all."

"And how are you coping with your be-reavement?" asked Charles.

Her face hardened. "I have hired a top psychiatrist to explain to the police that my poor son was brutalised and traumatised into committing those terrible deeds. He should not be blamed."

"Gwen's getting help from a good thera-pist," said Gareth.

"Oh, she's ever so clever. She's just moved to the Cotswolds. Her name is Jill Davent."

"The one in Carsely?"

"Oh, yes. Do you know her?"

"I haven't met her."

"Oh, but you should," said Gwen sweetly. "Perhaps she could find out the deep reason you are not married."

"Perhaps she could," said Charles ami-ably. "Did you eat any of your late fiancé?"

"How dare you bring all that up?" said Gwen, beginning to cry.

"Get out of here!" roared Gareth.

"And that was that," said Charles after he had given his report to Agatha.

"What on earth prompted you to ask if she'd eaten any of John?" asked Agatha.

"It just came out," said Charles ruefully. "She looked so . . . well . . . smug. And that crack about me needing to visit this therapist really annoyed me. Let's go to the pub in Carsely. I could do with a drink."

In the Red Lion, they took their drinks out into the pub garden.

"I'm sure Gwen must have known what her son was up to," said Agatha.

"I don't think so," said Charles. "I mean, if Walt hadn't murdered John, then she would have married him."

"Just wish I could be a fly on the wall when she's talking to that therapist."

"Look! Here comes James," said Charles.

James walked into the pub garden, carrying two glasses. He was accompanied by a small woman. She had straight black hair and rather protuberant dark eyes set in a pug-like face.

Agatha waved to James as a signal to join them, but James only nodded and led his companion to a table a good bit away from them. Soon he and his companion were absorbed in deep conversation.

"Who the hell is she?" demanded Agatha fiercely.

"Whoever she is, our James does seem fascinated," said Charles.

"Can't possibly be," said Agatha sourly. "She looks like a constipated otter. I need another drink. Go into the bar and find out who she is."

"Yours to command," said Charles lazily.

When he came back, he said, "That is the therapist."

"What! The one Gwen is going to?"

"The same."

"I'll go and see her myself," said Agatha.

"Come on, Aggie. Butt out."

"I need to protect James. What can he see in her?"

When Charles eventually left, Agatha sat in her garden and fretted. She would not admit to herself that she was jealous.

By late afternoon, she felt she couldn't bear it any longer, picked up that flyer and phoned Jill.

"I would like to make an appointment," she said.

"What is your name?" asked the therapist.

"Agatha Raisin. I live in the village."

"I could see you in half an hour's time. I have had a cancellation." Her voice was husky and attractive.

"Okay," said Agatha, but suddenly feeling the whole idea of seeing this woman was stupid.

Jill ushered Agatha into what she called her consulting room. It was dark, as the blinds were drawn. There was a smell of joss. Agatha was told to sit in an armchair and Jill sat on a hard upright seat behind her.

"Now what is troubling you?" Jill asked.

"I am having nightmares," said Agatha.

"I can help with that. First let us go back into your childhood and start there. Tell me about it."

Agatha had no intention of telling this woman about her upbringing in a Birmingham slum, or about her alcoholic parents. So she invented an idyllic childhood in a Cotswold village and happy school days. Her father had been a farmer and her mother, an old-fashioned housewife. She was rambling on happily and had just got to the bit where her fictitious mother was making one of her famous chocolate cakes and letting little Agatha lick the spoon when Jill's voice interrupted her. "Don't tell me a load of lies, Mrs. Raisin, or I cannot help you."

Agatha leapt to her feet. "How dare you call me a liar."

"Only when necessary."

"I'm out of here," said Agatha. "You can take your therapy and stuff it up your scrawny arse."

"That will be sixty pounds."

"What!"

"That is my fee and I've earned it listening to your lies."

Face flaming, Agatha opened her wallet and threw three twenty-pound notes at Jill before storming out.

As she walked home, she wondered furiously how Jill had penetrated the layers and layers of middle class that she had lacquered herself with over the years.

She stopped short at the corner of Lilac Lane. James knew her background. Had James told her?

She strode to his cottage and banged on the door. There was no reply and his car was not parked outside.

Agatha was about to turn away when James drove up. He was no sooner out of his car than Agatha flew at him, shouting, "Did you tell her?"

He pushed her away and said, "You're gabbling. Tell who what?"

"That therapist. Did you tell her about my background?"

"What on earth are you talking about?" demanded James. "I never gossip about you."

"I'm sorry," said Agatha. "It's silly to be so ashamed of my background, but I am. I told her a fictitious tale about my childhood and she knew I was lying."

"Come in and have a coffee and tell me

why you went to her in the first place."

Agatha did not say she had been prompted by jealousy. Instead, she said that she had learned Gwen was consulting Jill and she wanted to see what sort of woman the therapist was.

"You saw me with her in the pub," said James. "You could have waited and asked me. I find her intelligent and sympathetic. She is a very good listener."

"So am I," said Agatha, "and I don't charge sixty pounds."

"I haven't been consulting her. I regard her as a friend."

"How did you meet her?"

"She called on me."

"Why?"

James looked awkward. "Jill said she was new to the village and wanted to meet a few interesting people. She had read my travel books."

"Wanted to meet a few unmarried men," said Agatha cynically.

"Let's talk about something else. Are you still suspicious of Gwen?"

"I am," said Agatha. "Very."

"Maybe you should trust the police on this one, Agatha. I am perfectly sure they grilled her."

"There's something about her that makes

men go weak at the knees," said Agatha.

"You need a break after all you've been through," said James. "Go on holiday."

"Maybe. I'll call on Bill Wong and see if there's any news."

It turned out to be Bill's day off. Once she got past the barrier of his formidable mother, Bill led her into the garden and listened to her suspicions about Gwen.

"We've got absolutely nothing on her," said Bill. "And believe me, we tried. Forensics went over that cold room where John was dissected. They found his fingerprints but none from Gwen so when she said she'd never ever go in there and left it all to her son, we had to believe her. Gareth Craven vouched for her and said she'd given up baking entirely after the murder of her husband."

"He's sweet on her," said Agatha. "I bet he'll be the next husband and God help him."

"Agatha, it's time to let go. You've had a dreadful experience. Forget it. Take a break. It's lovely weather."

Agatha sighed. "I'm maybe imagining things. I'll do that."

That evening, Jill had a visitor, but not a

client. Clive Tremund, a private detective from Oxford, accepted a cash payment and said, "Why were you so curious about the Raisin woman?"

"She's a detective. She lives here. I wanted to know all about her. She could make trouble for me and I'd like to keep her at arm's length."

"You mean you don't want her ferreting around in *your* background?"

"I've got nothing to hide. Now, get out of here."

Clive paused in the doorway. "I'd be careful if I were you. Murder follows that woman Raisin around."

"Pooh, it'll be a blue moon before anyone murders me."

After he had gone, Jill settled down in front of the television and switched on the news. Forest fires had been raging across Canada and a cloud of dust was heading across the Atlantic.

"So in our skies next week," said the announcer, "we may have the rare sight of a blue moon."

ABOUT THE AUTHOR

M. C. Beaton has been hailed as the "Queen of Crime" (*The Globe and Mail*). Chosen as the British Guest of Honor at Bouchercon 2006, she is the *New York Times* bestselling author of twenty-four previous Agatha Raisin novels, the Hamish Macbeth series, and an Edwardian mystery series. Born in Scotland, she currently divides her time between Paris and the English Cotswolds.

The employees of Thorndike Press hope you have enjoyed this Large Print book. All our Thorndike, Wheeler, and Kennebec Large Print titles are designed for easy reading, and all our books are made to last. Other Thorndike Press Large Print books are available at your library, through selected bookstores, or directly from us.

For information about titles, please call:
    (800) 223-1244

or visit our Web site at:
    http://gale.cengage.com/thorndike

To share your comments, please write:
    Publisher
    Thorndike Press
    10 Water St., Suite 310
    Waterville, ME 04901